CHORUS LIN

"The Happy Hoofers bring hilarity and hijinks to the high seas—or in this case, a Russian river cruise where murder is nothing to tap at. The cruise finds them kick-ball-changing and flap-kicking their way across Russia on a ship where murder points to more than a few unusual suspects."
Nancy Coco

"A fun read . . . the elements of hilarity and camaraderie between the characters make *Chorus Lines, Caviar, and Corpses* intriguing and worth the read."
RT Book Reviews

"A page-turning cozy mystery about five friends in their fifties dancing their way across Russia. From the first chapter, McHugh delivers. . . . The cast of characters includes endearing, scary, charming, crazy, and irresistible people. Besides murder and mayhem, we are treated to women who we might want as our best friends, our shrinks, and our travel companions."
Jerilyn Dufresne

"Featuring travel tips and recipes, this series debut features plenty of cozy adventure for armchair travelers and mystery buffs alike. Sue Henry and Peter Abresch fans will be delighted with this alternative."
Library Journal

"*Spasibo*, Mary McHugh—that's Russian for 'thank you.' *Chorus Lines, Caviar, and Corpses* is a huge treat for armchair travelers and mystery fans alike, as five spirited tap dancers cruise from St. Petersburg to Moscow undeterred by a couple of shipboard murders. Vivid description and deft touches of local color take the reader right along with them."

Peggy Ehrhart

"A fun book! Mary McHugh's *Chorus Lines, Caviar, and Corpses* is, quite literally, a romp. It has a little bit of everything, from tongue-in-cheek travel tips to romance and recipes (and, oh, are they *good*). Not even the most jaded reader will be able to resist plucky Tina Powell and her cadre of capering cougars aboard a cruise ship where death is on the menu, along with the caviar. What could be more delicious?"

Carole Bugge

"If you can't afford a Russian cruise up the Volga, this charming combination murder mystery travelogue, which mixes tasty cuisine and a group of frisky, wisecracking, middle-aged chorines, is the next best thing."

Charles Salzberg

"I just finished *Chorus Lines, Caviar, and Corpses*! Oh, WOW, was it great! I read it in less than two days. So good! Thank you for writing this book, and I can't wait till the next one!"

Shelley's Book Case

"I really enjoyed reading about the Happy Hoofers' trip on a Russian river cruise. This book had a lot of action. I learned a lot about Russia that I never knew before. Great job, Mary. I look forward to the next installment in the Happy Hoofers Mystery Series."
Melina's Book Blog

"I loved 'The Happy Hoofers' immediately. What a fun group. This mixes some of my favorite things in one book—a cruise ship setting, a group of friends, and a murder mystery. What could be better? This book moved along at a fast pace and had engaging characters—some nicer than others, of course. Add those things to a great setting and it's off on a wild adventure with a very interesting cast of characters."
Socrates' Book Review

FLAMENCO, FLAN, AND FATALITIES

"Flamenco, Flan, and Fatalities serves up just what it says: good entertainment, good food, and good mystery! I am looking forward to reading other books in this series."
Back Porchervations

"Talk about transporting the reader—I felt as if I were in Spain for the last few days."
Socrates Book Reviews

"It was fun to see how all the characters interacted and how their thought processes worked."
Laura's Interests

"You will laugh your way through this fantastic read. The characters are hilarious and the story line will keep you moving through the pages until the end."
Shelley's Book Case

"This is a first-time read for me by this author and I adored her book. . . . . The characters are a hoot."
Bab's Book Bistro

"I loved this book and reading about the great recipes included in the story. This book was full of adventure and mystery and had pulled me in and wouldn't let go!"
Community Bookstop

"*Flamenco, Flan, and Fatalities* is a lot of fun, a great read! I liked reading about the camaraderie of the five friends, and their sightseeing in Spain, just as much as trying to figure out *whodunit*. I really enjoyed it, and recommend *Flamenco, Flan, and Fatalities* to Cozy Mystery fans—armchair travelers, especially, will enjoy touring northern Spain on a luxury train with the Happy Hoofers."
Jane Reads

"A very humorous mystery with a key emphasis on friendship. There is a bit of romance, and the recipes are great too. This can be read as a stand-alone, but I recommend starting at the beginning with *Chorus Lines, Caviar, and Corpses*. They are quick, entertaining reads and a great way to spend an afternoon."
Escape With Dollycas Into a Good Book

CANCANS, CROISSANTS, AND CASKETS

"Armchair travelers and wannabe tap dancers will enjoy the series, especially since author McHugh employs the books to provide vicarious travel experiences, including the culinary delights of the current venue.
Tres magnifique!"
Mystery Scene Magazine

"This is a fast cozy murder and a clean read. It is entertaining. I will read more books from Mary McHugh in the future."
readalot

"I like how each book is told from a different Hoofer's perspective, which lets the readers get to know each Hoofer a little better."
Melina's Book Blog

"Not much dancing takes place in Paris, but oh the food! Sprinkled liberally through the book are recipes so good I believe I gained a few pounds while reading this mystery."
Laura's Interests

"A very entertaining read with some tempting recipes and some amusing travel tips are included throughout the book."
Escape With Dollycas Into A Good Book

"I love this series, and this book just cemented that opinion for me."
Book Babble

"All the characters are fun and whimsical, the story line is addictive and a total page turner. This book has everything a reader could ask for and more: There is humor, mystery, romance, friendship, a wonderful setting, and cute recipes."
LibriAmoriMiei

Also by Mary McHugh

The Happy Hoofers Mystery Series*
*Chorus Lines, Caviar, and Corpses**
*Flamenco, Flan, and Fatalities**
*Cancans, Croissants, and Caskets**
*Bossa Novas, Bikinis, and Bad Ends**

Cape Cod Murder
The Perfect Bride
The Woman Thing
Law and the New Woman
Psychology and the New Woman
Careers in Engineering and Engineering Technology
Veterinary Medicine and Animal Care Careers
Young People Talk about Death
Special Siblings: Growing up with Someone with a Disability
How Not to Become a Little Old Lady
How Not to Become a Crotchety Old Man
How to Ruin Your Children's Lives
How to Ruin Your Marriage
How to Ruin Your Sister's Life
Eat This! 365 Reasons Not to Diet
Clean This! 320 Reasons Not to Clean
Good Granny/Bad Granny
How Not to Act Like a Little Old Lady
If I Get Hit by a Bus Tomorrow, Here's How to Replace the Toilet Paper Roll
Aging with Grace—Whoever She Is
Go for It: 100 Ways to Feel Young, Vibrant, Interested and Interesting after 50

*Available from Kensington Publishing Corp.

High Kicks, Hot Chocolate, and Homicides

A Happy Hoofers Mystery

Mary McHugh

KENSINGTON PUBLISHING CORP.
http://www.kensingtonbooks.com

KENSINGTON BOOKS are published by

Kensington Publishing Corp.
119 West 40th Street
New York, NY 10018

All Kensington Titles, Imprints, and Distributed Lines are available at special quantity discounts for bulk purchases for sales promotions, premiums, fund-raising, and educational or institutional use. Special book excerpts or customized printings can also be created to fit specific needs. For details, write or phone the office of the Kensington special sales manager: Kensington Publishing Corp., 119 West 40th Street, New York, NY 10018, attn: Special Sales Department, Phone: 1-800-221-2647.

Kensington and the K logo Reg. U.S. Pat & TM Off.

ISBN-13: 978-1-4967-0376-7
ISBN-10: 1-4967-0376-6
First Kensington Mass Market Edition: October 2016

eISBN-13: 978-1-4967-0377-4
eISBN-10: 1-4967-0377-4
First Kensington Electronic Edition: October 2016

10 9 8 7 6 5 4 3 2 1

Printed in the United States of America

To New York, the most exciting city in the world

Chapter 1

Rock On Rockettes

"**W**hat do you mean you're going to dance with the Rockettes?" George said, buttering his croissant and holding out his cup for more coffee.

"It's true," I said. "We're going to be part of their Christmas show."

"But they're professionals," he said.

"So are we, George," I said. "People pay us to dance. That makes us professionals."

"Mary Louise, you're a housewife," he said. "Your job is here, taking care of this house. Taking care of me."

I looked at this man I'd been married to for thirty years and wondered if he knew me at all. I had been dancing on cruise ships and trains and in hotels for the past couple of years with my friends Tina, Janice, Gini, and Pat. We call ourselves the Happy Hoofers. Our names have been all over the TV and newspapers because we've solved a few murders here and there. We are really good dancers, and Tina, our leader, gets more offers for jobs than we can accept.

Did I still love George? Sometimes I wasn't sure. I thought I was in love with Mike Parnell, the doctor I met when we danced on a luxury train in northern Spain. His wife Jenny had died two years before, and he was lost without her. I have the same dark hair and blue eyes she had, and he fell in love with me. Not just because I looked like Jenny, but he thought I was like her in other ways too. He said I was kind to people who didn't deserve it, that I always made people feel good about themselves, that I looked at life as an adventure. I tried not to love him back, but after that trip I seriously considered leaving George for him. Mike was so much fun, so interesting, so good to me.

That was the part that got me, I think. He was always thinking of me and what would make me happy. George was always thinking of how I could make him happy. I tried to excuse him by reminding myself that he had his own law practice in New Jersey, that he was overworked and tired a lot of the time.

Then I thought of Mike, an obstetrician, and pictured him delivering babies at all hours of the night. He worked just as hard as George, but he still put me first. *Let it go. Mary Louise, let it go,* I told myself. I was brought up to believe that you should hang in there, even when marriage wasn't so great. That all marriages go through bad patches.

The kitchen door swung open and Tucker, our golden retriever, loped in and bumped his face on my leg. I gave him a hug.

"Hey Tucker," I said. "Hungry?"

He wagged his tail so vigorously he almost whacked George on the leg.

I filled Tucker's bowl with the dry stuff he loved and filled his water dish.

My cell rang. It was Tina Powell, the editor of a bridal magazine, and the leader of our Happy Hoofers dance troupe. We've been friends forever, since the days we worked at *Redbook* magazine together and the crazy trip we took across the country in a beat-up old car.

"Hi, Weezie," she said. Only my closest friends are allowed to call me that. "Ready to meet the Rockettes? We're supposed to show up at Radio City Music Hall this morning for a backstage tour. Peter's going to drive us into the city. Can you believe we're going to dance with them? The Rockettes!"

"No," I said. "I still don't believe it," I said. "Tell me again why they're letting us do this."

"Just to have something different in their Christmas show this year. We're only going to be a brief part of their program. We're dancing to 'Santa Claus is Coming to Town,' and we're wearing very short Santa outfits with Santa hats. We come out on the stage alone and then all the Rockettes join us."

"It's incredible, Tina. What time are we leaving?"

"We'll pick you up at nine. Oh, and bring your tap shoes."

"We're going to dance this morning?"

"I think they want to see how much training we need."

"I can tell them," I said. "A lot."

"See you at nine, hon," Tina said and hung up.

The idea of performing with the Rockettes on the stage of Radio City was so exciting I practically danced to the sink with the breakfast dishes.

"You're going into the city today?" George asked. "I thought you were going to get the car washed."

"Oh George, I can do that any time," I said. "This is a chance to meet the Rockettes for the first time. Tina thought we might get the chance to dance a little today, but she wasn't sure."

I rinsed off the plates and juice glasses and stuck them in the dishwasher.

"Well, I hope you don't plan to spend much time in the city." George said. "There's a lot to do around here with Christmas coming."

"It's only October," I said, my happy mood disappearing down the drain. "I don't even have to think about shopping and the tree and all that until the end of November. You should be glad I'm not in Thailand or some place like that. I'll only be across the river in New York. I can get a lot of the stuff I need there."

"Just be sure you're back here in time for dinner," he said, rattling his *New York Times* noisily.

Maybe, maybe not, I thought, leaving the room

to get my tap shoes. I gave the shoes a quick shine and popped them into my bag. How I loved those little shoes. Because of them I had traveled to Russia, Spain, Paris, and Rio. I had tapped, flamencoed, sambaed, and cariocaed.

Dancing to me was like being set free to whirl out into space, to let go of all my inhibitions and let my body lead me wherever it wanted to go. When I danced, I forgot George and New Jersey and even my children. I wasn't Mary Louise Temple any more. I was a shooting star, a sparkling rocket, a flash of light. I hugged my bag with the shoes in them against my chest and did a couple of twirls around the room.

George walked into the room at that moment and smiled.

"You're beautiful," he said and kissed me.

"Thank you, sweetheart," I said. "I won't be late. I'm cooking your favorite dinner tonight—salmon and anchovies."

"I may be a little late," he said. "The Alderson case is taking longer to prepare for than I thought."

"Tell me again what that case is about," I said, trying to comb the curl out of my hair. I wanted that nice straight look everybody else had, but my hair always rebelled and popped out with a little wiggle whenever it got the chance.

"This woman is suing the company because her husband stepped into an empty elevator shaft in the building they own and was killed."

"That's horrible!" I said. "How do you defend that?"

"It was obviously the fault of the company

that built the elevator, not the company that owned the building. The door shouldn't open onto an empty shaft, but it did. It's a complicated case, though, and it's a lot of work."

He looked preoccupied, worried. I had a glimpse into the long hours he spent with each case because of his care and perfectionism.

"You'll do a great job," I said. "You always do."

He smiled his thanks at me and hugged me.

I gave him a quick kiss and went downstairs to wait for Tina and the others.

At nine, right on the dot, Peter's car pulled into our driveway. I like Peter a lot. He makes Tina happy. He had been her husband Bill's law partner, and he and his wife had been close friends of theirs while Bill was alive. Then Peter and Helen divorced, and a couple of years later, Bill died of brain cancer.

Peter did everything to help Tina adjust to life without Bill. He was especially good with her children. He helped them choose a college and drove them there in the fall and went with Tina to pick them up in the spring. He took her out to dinner every chance he got. He drove her to planes when she had to travel for business. He fell in love with her in the process. For a long time Tina just thought of him as a good friend, but gradually she grew to love him too. They kept talking about getting married, but somehow Tina was always off somewhere dancing instead of arranging the wedding. She was lucky that Peter was such a patient man.

Now that we were going to be in New York for a while, I hoped she would stop putting the wedding off and do it. Tina wanted the reception to be in the Frick Museum in New York, one of my favorite places in the world, as well as hers, because it was so much like a home as well as a museum. I could always picture the Fricks living there. Knowing Tina, it would be an exquisitely beautiful reception.

I ran outside and hopped in the van where the rest of my Hoofer friends were already ensconced. Somehow all four of us fitted in the back seat with plenty of room to sip our coffee and munch on the rolls that Peter had supplied.

"Hey, Weezie," Peter said. "I hear you're going to be a Rockette."

"Is that crazy or what?" I said. "How Tina talked them into letting us dance on that huge stage at Christmas time with all those perfect Rockettes, I'll never know."

"Didn't you know?" Peter said with a loving glance at Tina sitting next to him in the front seat. "Tina can do anything."

"Except plan her own wedding," Gini Miller, our documentary filmmaker Hoofer, said in her usual in-your-face mode.

"Gini," Tina said, her voice low, warning.

"Oh, Gini, shut up," Janice Rogers said, using her stage director voice instead of her usual gentle one.

"Let's not talk about that right now, Gini," Pat, our peace-making family-therapist Hoofer said, dispelling the threat of a quarrel before we even got out of the driveway.

Peter backed the van into the street and headed for Route 24 that led to Route 78, which would take us through the Lincoln Tunnel and into the city to Rockefeller Center. Peter was an excellent driver and maneuvered his vehicle in and out of the morning traffic with skill and expertise.

"So, Tina, what's happening today?" Pat asked, choosing a safe subject.

"Well, Glenna, the head Rockette, was a little vague," Tina said, "but I got the impression that they just wanted to meet us, introduce us to the Rockettes, give us a tour of the theater, and tell us what we will be doing in the show."

"Why are we bringing our tap shoes?" I asked.

"I'm not sure," Tina said. "But I think they want to be sure we can really dance."

"Of course we can dance!" Gini said impatiently. "What do they think we were doing in Rio—directing traffic?"

"Almost getting killed," Pat muttered with a little shudder.

I put my arm around her for a second in a gesture of sympathy. She had been through a terrifying time in Brazil.

Tina reached over the seat and squeezed Pat's hand. "They knew we were dancing in Rio," she said, "but they want to be sure we can really tap their way. We mostly flung ourselves around doing the samba and the bossa nova in Brazil. It's not the kind of disciplined dancing the Rockettes do."

"Think we can do it?" Janice asked.

"With a lot of work," Tina said. "And I mean long hours of rehearsal."

George will have a fit, I thought, and then, *Tough!* I seemed to be having such ambivalent feelings about him lately since I met Mike. I needed to talk to somebody about it. Pat was the logical choice. She's a wonderful therapist. I would talk to her. She always helped. I glanced over at her with a querying look. She read my mind.

"Will George be okay with long hours away from your wifely duties, Mary Louise?" she asked.

"He'll have to be," I said. "He has no choice."

"There's always a middle way," she said, "Life isn't just black or white, perfect or not perfect."

"Can we talk?" I said, and my understanding friends chuckled. They all knew how much Pat helped us when we had problems. Every one of us had turned to her in times of crisis. She was always wise and insightful.

"Any time, hon," she said.

Peter emerged from the Lincoln Tunnel, wove his way to Sixth Avenue and Fiftieth Street and let us out in front of Radio City Music Hall.

"Give me a call when you're ready to leave," he said to Tina. "And I'll come pick you up"

"We might only be here a short time, Peter," she said. "Don't worry about us. We'll take the train home."

"Call me anyway," he said. "I can usually work something out."

I wished George had such a flexible schedule in his firm as Peter had. George never seemed to be able to "work something out" even though he was the main partner of the firm.

We thanked Peter and followed Tina into Radio City.

"May I help you?" the ticket taker said.

"We're the Happy Hoofers," Tina said. "We're looking for Glenna Parsons. We're going to be working with her."

The ticket taker, who looked about fifteen, said, "You're going to be Rockettes?" He tried, but he couldn't hide his disbelief that women our age could possibly be Rockettes. We're only in our early fifties, but to him, we must have seemed ancient.

"You bet we are," Gini said. I love Gini. She always says what the rest of us don't have the nerve to say. "They're begging us to join them. Want to tell Glenna we're here?"

He fumbled with his phone and then clicked a button.

"M-m-m-s Parsons," he said, "they're here. Them," he said after a pause. "You know, those Happy Hookers. They're here." People often call us that to tease us, but this boy just made an honest mistake. I think.

Tina gently pried the phone out of his hands.

"Glenna?" she said. "It's Tina. I brought my gang as you requested. We're dying to meet the Rockettes. Where do we go next?"

Tina listened to the answer and then said to us, "She's meeting us on the stage. We ought to be able to find that without any problem."

She handed the phone back to the flustered young man and motioned to the rest of us to follow her into the theater. My first sight of that magnificent foyer brought back the memory of coming to this theater when my children were little. I used to come here while they were in school. In those days, you could see a feature movie, some cowboy short films, a stage show—with the Rockettes of course—and a comedy skit.

I would go into the theater about eleven o'-clock in the morning and snuggle down in my comfortable seat. I'd pretend I didn't have to go back to my housewifey world. That I could just stay there totally immersed in the feature movie, dancing with them, singing with them, worrying about some incredibly silly problem that of course was solved in ninety minutes. Then I'd stumble out of there around two o'clock and go back home in time to greet my children when they came home from school.

It was heaven. I always came back home refreshed, entertained, calm and ready to cook some more meals, wash some more dishes, pick up stuff all over the house, and drive my children wherever they needed to go after school. I had two boys and a girl and raising them was the best job I ever had and the hardest work.

Two of them are in college now and one in law school, but I wouldn't have traded those years for anything. Radio City was a blessed respite. I still felt that way as I looked at the huge mural on the wall next to the staircase leading up to the balcony showing a man searching for the fountain of youth. Or at least that's what I always thought he was doing.

I followed Tina and the others through the impressive gold doors up the long aisle to the huge stage. Someone once told me the stage was meant to represent the sunrise with enormous gold arches framing it. Everything in this vast theater built by Samuel L. Rothafel that seated six thousand people was planned to suggest joy and a new day full of promise and fun.

We clambered onto the stage and an attractive woman with dark hair pulled back into a twist, long legs, and a wide smile, hurried out of the wings to greet us.

"Welcome, Hoofers," she said. "I'm Glenna. We are so glad you're going to join us for our Christmas show."

"Hello, Glenna," Tina said and introduced each of us.

Glenna looked us over, and we could see her planning make-up, hair arrangements, costume sizes for each one of us in her mind. She seemed happiest when she turned her attention to Janice, but we're all used to that.

She wouldn't have to do much for Janice because she was so beautiful. Effortlessly beautiful. We'd all hate her if she weren't one of the world's nicest people. Kind, loving, totally unimpressed with her beauty. She just thought of it as something she inherited—like good teeth or nice hair or young skin. Nothing she should be proud of or ashamed of. Useful in the theater. It was just there. And it got us lots of jobs, to be crass about it. Producers took one look at Janice and hired us on the spot.

Actually, we're all pretty good-looking. Because of the hours we spend dancing, we're slim and in good shape. If it weren't for that, I'd probably sit home and eat chocolate peanut butter Häagen-Dazs ice cream until I weighed a hundred and fifty pounds. We also have great legs, but that wasn't really because of dancing. We just inherited them from mothers or grand-mothers with smashing gams.

"The Rockettes do their own hair and makeup," Glenna said. "But I thought you might like a little help since you're not used to our system. The girls only wear lipstick, fake eyelashes, and fix their hair in a French twist. They're used to it and can do it really fast. Would you like one of us to give you a little help?"

We all nodded vigorously, me especially. I couldn't imagine turning into a Rockette with "lipstick, fake eyelashes, and a French twist." My own hair pretty much resisted being pulled back and tied up. And lipstick and fake eyelashes weren't going to do it. I needed a lot more than that. Was she kidding?

"That would be great, Glenna," Tina said, speaking for all of us. "What about our costumes?"

"Well, as you know, you're going to do the Santa bit, and the costumes weigh about 40 pounds! Think you can dance with that?"

"Forty pounds!" Gini said. "What the heck are they made of—lead?"

Fortunately, Glenna laughed. We're never sure how people are going to react to Gini. We're used to her, but not everyone appreciates her comments.

"It has a fat round ball inside it so you'll look like Santa with his big tummy," she said. "But maybe we can work something else out and get lighter costumes for you guys."

"That would be good," Tina said. "Anything you can do to make it easier for us would be wonderful. We want to be like the Rockettes, but I don't think we can ever actually *be* the Rockettes."

"Not to worry," Glenna said. "We'll get you as close to us as we can. Mostly it's rehearse, rehearse, rehearse, and exercise, exercise, exercise. Are you ready for that?"

"You bet," Tina said. "When do you want us to start?"

"Not 'til tomorrow," Glenna said. "Today, I want you to meet the rest of the Rockettes."

"How many are there?" Pat asked.

"Eighty all together, but there are only thirty-six on stage at any one time. With you, there will be forty-one."

Glenna clicked a number on her phone and said, "Send 'em in, please, Annie."

The sound of all those tap shoes clickety-clacking down the stairs and onto the stage sounded like an army lining up for inspection. We were soon surrounded by what seemed like thousands of pretty young women even though there were only eighty. They were smiling and friendly and amazingly lively for that hour of the morning.

"Ladies," Glenna said, "I want you to meet Tina, Gini, Janice, Pat, and Mary Louise. They're the Happy Hoofers. They're going to dance the Santa Claus number with us."

"Lots of luck dancing in jackets that weigh forty pounds," one woman said.

She was one of the taller Rockettes. I knew that you had to be between five feet six inches and five feet ten and a half inches tall to be one of the Rockettes. She must have been about five ten. Her legs alone looked five eight. She had blond hair, highlighted with lighter streaks. She must have been about twenty-five years old, but her face was hard. She didn't smile when she commented on the Santa costumes.

"Knock it off, Marlowe," Glenna said. "I already told them we'd take the fat out of the suits to make them lighter. Stop trying to scare them. They're going to be a delightful addition to our Christmas show."

"If we have to dance in those things with the fat in, they should have to wear them that way too," Marlowe said, still unsmiling.

"Audiences are used to seeing us like that," Glenna said. "It's a tradition. But our Hoofers here can probably get away without the extra addition."

She looked around at her whole group of Rockettes. "Can I count on you guys to help these Hoofers become temporary Santas?"

Loud shouts of "Sure," and "You bet," and "Of course," from all those super-thin, stunning dancers made us feel great. I noticed Marlowe didn't join in the generally helpful shouts. She just stared at us unsmiling.

"OK," Glenna said, ignoring Marlowe. "Let's show them what we'll be doing. Line up and do your stuff." She switched on the music that would be played by a real orchestra for the actual performance.

"When we perform," she continued, "we wear little microphones attached to the backs of our heels to make the tapping louder. You will too. Otherwise people in the back row would miss that great sound."

Microphones on our shoes! I could see this would be unlike any dancing we had ever done before.

We moved off the stage to watch as the Rockettes lined up and swung into the routine for "Santa Claus is Coming to Town." They kicked higher than I could ever imagine doing. This was going to take a lot more work than I had dreamed. But we were going to be Rockettes! Or as close to them as we could manage.

When they finished, we jumped to our feet and applauded.

"Think you can do that?" Glenna asked.

"We'll knock ourselves out trying," Tina said.

We all had questions for Glenna.

"When do we start?" Gini said.

"How long will it take us to learn how to dance like they do?" Pat asked.

"What time will we finish rehearsing?" I asked. The memory of George's *Be home in time for dinner* echoed in my mind.

"Do we get a lunch break?" Janice asked. Somehow she managed to eat all the time and never gain an ounce. I could read her mind, though, and knew she wanted to plan some lunches with her boyfriend Tom in her favorite city in the world. I sort of hoped I could sneak in some

time with Mike when he wasn't delivering somebody's baby. Lunch was harmless enough.

"We rehearse every day—not weekends—from
ten in the morning until five in the evening,"
Glenna said. "But we have a lot more routines
than you have. We have eight costume changes
with every performance and we do five shows a
day. You only wear the Santa outfit, and you're
all through after that part of the show."

That was a relief. I couldn't imagine doing
what they did. These Rockettes were incredible.

"You won't spend the whole rehearsal time
dancing, though." Glenna continued. "You'll
have an hour-long workout of push-ups, leg
raises, running in place—lots of things like that.
Then you'll spend the rest of the time practicing the dancing. It's not easy what we do."

"Do you want us to start today?" Tina asked.

"No, today is just a meet-and-greet," Glenna
said. "We start tomorrow. Can you get here by
ten again?"

"Absolutely," Tina said.

"See you tomorrow, then," Glenna said. "I
just got a call about the timing of the descent of
the stage. It hasn't been lowered at the right
time in the last couple of rehearsals. I've got to
go check on it. There's always something." She
waved and walked off the stage.

We said goodbye to her and walked out to the
entrance of the theater.

Outside, Tina said, "Want me to call Peter to
take us home? Or do you want to spend the day
in the city now that we're here?"

We all talked at once telling her we wanted to stay in New York for the day.

I'm going up to the Frick to start making arrangements for my wedding reception after we finish the Christmas show. Sometime in January maybe," Tina said. "I'll see what's available."

"Think I'll run over to the *Times* and see if Alex is free for lunch and find out what's going on in the city today," Gini said. Alex Boyer was an editor at *The New York Times*. Gini met him when we danced on a cruise ship in Russia. He was bureau chief of the Moscow office at that time, and the two of them hit it off right away.

Alex loved to travel as much as Gini did. He also admired her work. He was impressed with the prize-winning documentary she made about Hurricane Katrina in New Orleans. Gini had divorced her husband several years before she met Alex because he wanted her to stay home and clean the house. That wasn't the life for our adventurous friend so she left him. Alex was perfect for her. When he heard she was trying to adopt Amalia, a little girl she met in India while she was doing a film on the orphanages in that country, he volunteered to help her.

The Indian government made it very difficult for a foreigner to adopt a child in their country. Alex promised to use his resources at the *Times* to find out how she could do that. Gini was obviously as much in love with Alex as he was with her, but she was wary of getting married again. For now, they did everything together except say

"I do" at the altar. I don't think I've ever seen Gini so happy.

"I'm going to meet Tom," Janice said. "It's Monday, so he doesn't have to perform today. I'm going to see if he'll go to Governor's Island with me. I've always wanted to go there. There's an exhibit of interactive sculpture there now—whatever that is. We want to find out. We can eat at that restaurant in Battery Park and then take the ferry over to the island."

"Sounds like fun," Tina said. "Enjoy, Jan."

Pat said she was going to have lunch with Denise, the woman she lived with in New Jersey, who worked at a public relations firm in New York.

"I don't often get to see Denise during the week since she's in the city and I'm home counseling clients," she said. "This will be a special treat for us." She clicked on her phone to make the call.

"What about you, Weezie?" Tina said. "Want to come to the Frick with me? I know you love that museum."

"No thanks, Tina," I said. "I want to eat in some restaurant by the water."

I really wanted to have lunch with Mike, but I didn't mention it to my friends. It didn't seem right to see him again, but I knew I would call him. I loved talking to him, and I wanted to tell him about the Music Hall. He got a big kick out of everything I did, the nuttier the better.

"Bye then, everyone," Tina said. "Let's meet here around five and Peter will take us home."

"See ya," Gini said, heading toward the *Times* building.

When they had all scattered in different directions, I called Mike.

"Hey, love," he said. "When's your baby due?"

I laughed. He always makes me laugh. He never starts a conversation asking me why I didn't do something I was supposed to do or why I did do something I wasn't supposed to do.

"Hi Mike," I said. "I'm in New York. Can you believe we're going to dance with the Rockettes?"

"I can believe anything you five Hoofers do," he said. "Will I get to see you?"

"Any chance you've got a free minute or two to meet me for lunch or a walk or something? We don't actually have to start rehearsals until tomorrow."

"I have more than a minute or two," he said, his voice reflecting his pleasure in hearing from me unexpectedly. "Let's meet at The Boathouse restaurant in the park for lunch." How did he know I wanted to eat by the water? The same way he always guessed what I really wanted to do.

"Sounds lovely," I said. "When?"

"Immediately," he said. "Grab a cab and meet me there as soon as you can. I can't wait to see you."

I found a taxi right away, which took me through Central Park to the entrance to The Boathouse restaurant with tables on the veranda that looked out on the water at people paddling rowboats away from the shore. Most of them didn't really know what they were doing so there were accidental bumps against other boats as the rowers struggled to move in the right direction down the lake.

Nobody got hurt. One little boy about four yelled to his mother as she rowed away from the dock, "This is the most fun I've ever had in my whole life." There was a lot of laughter, but I was glad I would be sitting on a non-moving chair watching them instead of competing against them

Mike was already there when my cab pulled up. He scooped me out of my seat, paid the driver and held me tight until we were seated at a table next to the railing overlooking the pond.

"Don't you have any babies to deliver or new mothers to advise or something medical you're supposed to be doing?" I asked when we were sitting across from each other.

"Nobody is even due today," he said. "Why haven't you called me, Mary Louise?"

"Oh Mike, you know why," I said.

"I know why, but I don't accept it," he said. "You know I love you. I'll always love you. And if you won't leave George, I still want to see you because you love me too even if you won't admit it now. You told me you loved me in Spain."

"Mike," I said, "try to understand. George and I have been married for thirty years. I can't throw those years away just like that. And it would hurt my children if I left him."

"They're grown. Or almost grown," he said. "They would learn to accept it."

"Don't ask me to leave him, Mike," I said. "Please don't. I know it's unfair of me to keep seeing you like this when I'm not going to leave George, but I can't help it. I love being with you, talking to you. You make me laugh. You make me feel good about myself. George has forgotten how to do that. Couldn't we just be friends?"

"Of course we can be friends," he said, holding my hand in his. "For now, I'll settle for a lunch whenever you're in New York."

I smiled.

"What's funny?" he asked.

"Well, the truth is, I'm going to be in New York every day until January," I said. "We're dancing with the Rockettes in their Christmas show."

"Every day?" he said, obviously delighted. "You're kidding!"

"What if some woman decides to have her baby in the middle of the day?" I asked.

"She'll just have to wait," he said. I knew he was kidding. He was the most caring, conscientious doctor I had ever met. He truly cherished the women who came to him to deliver their babies. They worshipped him.

"I don't even know if they're going to give us time to eat a real lunch," I said. "We're going to be rehearsing and exercising and Rocketting for hours every day."

"Just the fact that you're in the city every day," he said, "means that we can have some time together, babies and rehearsal times permitting."

The waiter hovered. "Want a drink?" Mike asked me.

"Maybe a glass of white wine," I said.

"Let's make it a Kir Royale," he said, remembering my favorite drink, Champagne with crème de cassis, from when we met in Spain.

I hesitated. *Oh why not?* "Sure," I said. "I don't have to dance or drive today."

"How was Rio?" he asked when the waiter went off to get our drinks. "I haven't really had a chance to hear about it since you got back."

"Except for a murder or three it was beautiful," I said. "Have you ever been there? I forget."

"Jenny and I went there on our honeymoon," he said. "We stayed at the Copacabana. Gorgeous hotel."

"That's where we were," I said. "And it's still gorgeous."

The waiter brought our drinks and asked if we had decided on lunch.

"What's good here, Mike?" I asked.

"Everything," he said. "Why don't you get an omelet or their quiche, which is excellent, or a salad. They have a great lobster salad here too."

"I love lobster," I said. "That's what I'll have."

Mike raised his glass. "Here's to lunch with you every day of my life when I'm not delivering a baby," he said.

I clinked my glass against his and took a sip. It was lovely. I looked out at the rowboats gliding along the lake. I changed my mind. I wanted to join them. "Oh Mike, do you think we could go for a rowboat ride when we finish lunch? I did that with my children when they were little, but I haven't done it since they grew up."

"Sure," he said. "You can row."

I laughed. "You think you're kidding," I said. "I'm actually a good rower."

"Is there anything you're not good at?" he asked.

"Just about everything else," I said.

Our lunches came and I took a bite of the lobster salad, which was perfect. Fat pieces of lobster, not the stringy insides you sometimes get in other restaurants, tangy bits of scallion, chopped up hardboiled eggs, a little tabasco to give it zing.

"I'm making this when the kids are home for Christmas vacation," I said. "Do you think you could persuade them to give me the recipe?"

Mike motioned to the waiter.

"Carlo, do you think you could get this recipe for madame here?" he said. "She's determined to steal it from you."

"Of course, Señor Mike," the waiter said. "I'll be right back."

As he left to get the recipe, my phone vibrated. I usually don't answer my phone when I'm with another person. I think it's rude. But something made me answer this call.

It was Tina. "Mary Louise?" she said. "You won't believe this, but Glenna—you know, the Rockette who was in charge this morning?—she's dead."

I almost dropped my phone in the lake. "What do you mean she's dead?" I said. "What happened to her?"

"They found her under the stage, mangled in the machinery."

"My God," I said. "How did that happen?"

"Nobody knows. The police are there now,

and we have to return to the theater. The detective wants to talk to us."

"How soon?"

"As soon as you can get back here. Where are you?"

"At The Boathouse," I said.

"With Mike?" she asked. Tina knows everything.

"As a matter of fact—" I started to say.

"Never mind," she said. "Just get back here as soon as you can."

"What's the matter?" Mike asked when I put my phone back in my purse.

"You won't believe this," I said. "But one of the Rockettes—the one we met this morning—is dead."

Our mood of festivity was gone. "Come on, I'll take you back to the theater. We'll take that rowboat ride another time."

He took a sip of the Kir Royale, left money on the table, got the recipe from the waiter, and led me out to the street where there were cabs waiting.

RECIPE FOR LOBSTER SALAD

Serves 2

1 lb. cooked lobster meat
3 radishes, chopped
3 T. chopped scallions
3 T. chopped celery
3 T. mayonnaise
2½ tsp. lemon juice (fresh—don't use the
    bottled stuff)
⅛ tsp. Tabasco sauce
2 hard-boiled eggs
2 hot dog rolls
Romaine lettuce leaves

1. Mix the first seven ingredients in a bowl, and add salt and pepper to taste.
2. Chop up the eggs and fold them carefully into the salad.
3. Fill the hot dog rolls with the lobster salad and place them on the lettuce leaves. You know, tastefully, as if for a ladies' lunch. Then forget the ladies part and gobble up the lobster salad.

Mary Louise's cooking tip: Lots of people say they don't like anchovies, so don't tell them you put them in this dish. They'll never know the difference.

Chapter 2

Home, Sour Home

Several police cars were parked in front of the theater.

"I'm coming in with you," Mike said as we got out of the cab.

I didn't argue with him. I wanted him there. I needed his strength and keen mind to help me stay calm.

The policeman at the entrance checked off my name on his list and let Mike in at my request.

The detective was a very tall black man,

handsome, wearing glasses, gray-haired. He motioned to us to come up on the stage, which was crowded with what looked like all eighty Rockettes and my four friends.

"Mrs. Temple?" he said when I climbed the steps onto the stage.

"Yes," I said, "And this is my friend, Dr. Parnell."

"Are you here to examine the body, Doctor?" the detective asked. "It's no longer here in the theater."

"No, no, detective," Mike said. "I'm an obstetrician, a friend of Mrs. Temple's. I was with her when she heard the news."

"Where is the body?" Gini asked.

"The EMTs took her to Bellevue."

"Was she still alive?" Gini asked.

"No, but the medical examiner is making out his report there."

"They told us she was mangled in the machinery under the stage," Gini said. "How did that happen? What was she doing under there? How could she have fallen like that?"

"We're here to find out the answers to all those questions," the detective said.

Mike said to me in a low voice, "I'm going back to the hospital. I'll see you tomorrow."

I nodded, and he walked back up the aisle and out of the theater.

The detective turned to face everyone on the stage and motioned to all of us to quiet down so he could speak to us. But before he could say anything, the sweetest cat with a white furry body, a beigey-blond face, and a long striped tail, rubbed up against his leg and mewed. I think she was what is called a creamsicle tabby. The detective looked down and smiled. He leaned over and picked up the little cat and said, "And who do we have here?"

"That's Ranger," one of the other Rockettes said. She was brown-skinned, stunningly beautiful, and wore long silver earrings I wanted to steal right out of her ears. "She's our mascot. Somebody left her here in the theater one time, and we adopted her."

The detective patted Ranger, rubbed his face against hers and handed her back to the woman with the earrings. He straightened up, put on his policeman's face and addressed us.

"I'm Detective Carver," he said. "I'm here to investigate this case. I would like to talk to each of you." He looked around at the huge crowd in front of him. "Which might take a while," he continued. "Anything you can tell me about Glenna Parsons will be very helpful. Please be available when we call you."

Marlowe, the Rockette who commented on the Santa outfits when we were on the stage earlier in the day with Glenna, spoke up. "Detective, will this take very long? We're supposed to start rehearsal in a few minutes in a church near here."

I remembered that Glenna had told us they rehearsed in a church with a large stage instead of in the theater.

"You may leave," Carver said. "Just tell one of

my men where the church is and how long you'll be there. We'll question you after the rehearsal."

As Marlowe and the other Rockettes headed toward the exit, Tina stopped her. "Do you want us to rehearse with you in the church now?" she asked.

"No," she said. "Just be here tomorrow morning at ten. A couple of the other Rockettes and I will show you what to do and practice with you."

She didn't seem all that eager to help us. Downright unfriendly, as a matter of fact.

Carver picked up Ranger again and addressed the five of us.

"I know you just met Ms. Parsons this morning," he said. "But do any of you have any information that might be helpful in our investigation?"

"I don't know if it means anything," Gini said, "but . . ."

"You'd be surprised at how much the smallest bit of information can matter," he said. "Please continue, Ms. Miller."

"Well," Gini continued, "as we left Glenna, she said something about having to check on the stage because it wasn't being lowered at the proper time."

The detective made a note on his iPad. "Interesting," he said. "Very interesting. Anything else you can remember that she said?"

"I think that's it," Gini said. "Oh, wait. She said she had gotten a call that there was something wrong with the timing device, and she was going to check on it."

"Did she say who the call was from?"

"I don't think so," Gini said and looked around at the rest of us questioningly.

"It was a very brief conversation, Detective," Tina said. "She hurried off, and we left the theater."

"Well, it gives me more to go on than I had before," the detective said. "Thank you, ladies." He patted Ranger and put her down next to her dish of food.

"Okay if we leave now, Detective?" Tina asked.

"Yes, of course," he said. "Thank you for your help."

We walked out to the foyer and took a sip of water from the art deco fountain.

"It's four o'clock," Tina said. "I don't know about the rest of you, but I'm ready to go home. I'll see if Peter can get away early if you want to leave too."

The wind had kind of gone out of my sails. I didn't feel like staying in the city any longer. A dead body under a stage can do that to you.

The rest of us nodded that we were ready to go home. Tina called Peter, who said he would pick us up in a few minutes. We went outside to wait for him.

"I don't like that Marlowe person," Janice said. Janice's instincts about people are almost never wrong. I didn't care for Marlowe either.

"We don't have to like her," Tina said. "We just have to learn from her. This is going to be the most difficult kind of dancing we've ever done, but we can do it, gang. We just have to rehearse a lot and do exactly what she tells us to do."

"Tina's right," Gini said. "But I don't like her either."

"I think the feeling is mutual," Janice said. "She didn't seem to want us around. What did we ever do to her?"

"Nothing, Jan," Pat said. "Some people just approach the world with a defensive attitude. It's like a protection for them. You know, a way of saying, 'Don't mess with me.'"

"Well, she better not mess with me," Gini said.

Tina punched her lightly on the arm. "Who'd mess with you, you vicious monster?" she said. We all laughed. Gini is the smallest of the five of us, with red hair and a gorgeous body.

Peter's van pulled up to the curb. We climbed into his comfortable vehicle and thanked him for coming to rescue us.

Peter edged out into the traffic and said over his shoulder, "Check out that ice chest on the floor, ladies. Margaritas and some quiches in there. Thought you might need them. I also put a Shirley Temple in there for Pat." It was so typical of Peter to remember that Pat had given up drinking.

"Thanks Peter," Pat said. "I barely had time for a sip of water in the restaurant with Denise when I got Tina's call and had to come back to the theater."

"Tom and I had a delicious lunch at an outdoor restaurant in Battery Park and were just about to get on the boat for Governor's Island when Tina called me," Janice said. "I still want to go there, though. And Pat, you might want to come with us and bring Denise's son David. There's interactive sculpture for children there. Grownups like it too."

"Great idea, Jan," Pat said. "David would love that."

"Hang on, Hoofers," Peter said. "We're off."

We attacked the chest and pulled out the drinks and quiches, grateful to Peter for his thoughtfulness. He was such a kind man. Like Mike. I always seemed to come back to thoughts of Mike when I thought of kindness. George used to be like that too.

"How was your Boathouse lunch with Mike?" Janice asked me. They must all know, I thought. Tina must have told them. Oh well, they're my friends. They'll understand.

"I had a great lobster salad," I said. "And I loved looking at the lake and all the people in rowboats. We were going to go out in a boat too when we finished lunch—Mike said I had to row—but then I got the call about Glenna. We're still going to do it. I'm actually a pretty good rower. I learned at camp when I was twelve."

"I'd rather just sit there and look at the water," Janice said. "It's so peaceful and soothing. Remember how much we loved eating in that restaurant on the lake in Spain, Gini?"

"That was fun," she said. "But the water in New York isn't exactly the cleanest. There are so many other things about this city that I like better—plays, movies, operas, symphonies . . ."

"Everything but murders," Janice said.

"Do me a favor, guys," I said. "Don't bring this subject up when you see George. It's hard enough getting out of the house every day to come into the city to rehearse. I'll tell him, but maybe not right away."

Peter inched the car forward in the line leading to the entrance into the Lincoln Tunnel. "Want me to talk to him, Mary Louise?" he asked. "You know, reassure him a little. I remember I didn't want Tina to dance on that train in Spain after she was almost killed in Russia, but I realized how much she loves dancing. I couldn't keep her from doing that. Maybe I can convince George how important it is to you."

"Oh Peter, would you?" I asked.

"Sure, I'll talk to him this evening when I bring you home."

"I'll be forever grateful if you can make him understand what this means to me. And you and Tina have to stay for dinner."

"I'd do anything for one of your dinners," he said. "It's a deal."

"What are you making?" Tina asked.

"Let's see," I said. "Tonight I think I'll make my salmon fillets. With garlic, anchovies, capers, lemon juice, and parsley. How does that sound?"

"Perfect," Peter said, moving the car forward a little more. "You just made me hungry. Could you hand me one of those quiches, please?"

I reached over the seat and put one of the delicious little ham and cheese quiches in his hand. They were bite-size so he gobbled it down and held out his hand for another, then took a sip from the bottle of water next to him.

"No more," he said when he had swallowed.

"Your salmon with anchovies are my favorites. I don't want to spoil my appetite."

We finally got through the tunnel and reached our town. Peter dropped Janice, Gini, and Pat off at their houses before stopping in front of our white Dutch Colonial house with the green shutters. I loved this house. It was full of light and all the things that were precious to me, from my children's first drawings to my grandmother's china and crystal.

George and I brought up our three children in this house. Two of them were in college now—Ellie in her freshman year at Princeton and Sam in his junior year at Northwestern. James was in his first year of Harvard Law School. After all those years in a house filled with laughter and music, I missed their noise and parties and the fun I had with them. I felt guilty now whenever I was glad to be free to go wherever I wanted, whenever I wanted, without having to hire a sitter.

They would all be home for Christmas vacation soon, and I'd be in New York rehearsing. It was all right, though, because they would rather be with their friends anyway. I was used to that. I could meet them in the city often. They were the great loves of my life. How would they feel if I left their father for Mike? They adored George. The more time I spent with Mike, the more I worried about my children's reactions to a divorce. But how could they not love Mike? Everybody loved him.

Peter parked in the driveway, and he and Tina and I went into my warm and welcoming house. George wasn't home yet. I noticed I felt relieved that I was there before he was. Come to think of it, I was usually more relaxed when he wasn't there. Not a good sign. Again, I realized how much I needed to talk to Pat.

Tucker bounded up to us when we opened the door. He was the best old dog. He didn't bark, just wagged his tail, looked as if he were smiling, and greeted us as if he had been waiting for us all day, which he probably had. He nuzzled Peter and Tina, who also loved him. This friendly dog would have welcomed anybody who came in the house, including thieves and rapists.

"Fix us some drinks, will you Peter?" I said. "You know where the bar is."

"I should after all these years," he said. "What'll you have, Weezie?"

"Make me a Manhattan, straight up, please. The sweet vermouth and the rye are in the bar on the top shelf. Oh, and the bitters are on the bottom shelf. Just a dash of those bitters, though, Peter. I like my Manhattans very sweet."

"Who drinks those things anymore anyway?" Peter said. "You might as well be living in an Agatha Christie murder mystery."

"Sometimes I feel like I am," I said.

"I just want a glass of white wine," Tina said. "A Sauvignon blanc, if you have it."

"I keep it here just for you," I said. "It's in the fridge."

"I'd rather have red," Peter said. "Okay if I steal a glass of your Pinot noir, Weez?"

"Of course, Peter," I said. "I'll go get the salmon ready while you do that."

I went into my lovely big kitchen, one of the main reasons I liked cooking so much. The stove top was in the center of a large granite counter in the middle of the room, the oven on the wall beside it. I had plenty of space on either side to chop, mince, shred, slice, and pummel stuff for the dishes I made. There were wide windows on one side of the room that looked out on my garden. It was next to a patio where I curled up on a padded chair and read on summer days when I wasn't dancing somewhere with my Hoofers.

A patch of herbs next to the back door was always ready to be snipped for whatever dish I was making that night. Some basil, some thyme, some oregano poked their sprouts up to flavor my dinners. The patio looked out on a lawn tended by Billy next door, now that my boys were away in school or working in the summertime. I had planted azalea bushes around the sides of the lawn and in front of our house. There were neat little clusters of asters and peonies near the patio. I would miss all that if I left this house to go live with Mike in the city.

I clicked open my iPad to the cooking app and pulled up the recipe for salmon with anchovies. I kept the iPad in a plastic bag to protect it from any splashing, spilling, or spattering that might go on while I cooked. I was an enthusiastic, free-ranging cook, so sometimes things got out of hand. I took the salmon fillets out of the fridge. Luckily I had two extras. I like to make two meals at a time, so the second is all ready to heat over for another dinner. This time I had two hungry guests to gobble them up. I always loved cooking for Tina and Peter because they were such enthusiastic munchers.

I softened enough butter for the four fillets in the microwave, mixed it with a can of anchovies, which I chopped up, a minced garlic clove, and a little salt and pepper. Then all I had to do was melt the anchovied, garlicy butter in a large pan that could go into the oven. I'd brown the salmon in the mixture, pop the pan into my 400-degree oven for a couple of minutes, add some capers and fresh lemon juice to the whole thing and serve. I'd make some rice and a salad to go with them, and I'd be all set. Easy and delicious. Even George liked this dish.

I went back into the living room, and Peter handed me a dark red Manhattan with a cherry at the bottom. He had even found the proper glass to put it in—a wide-mouthed martini glass. My grandfather used to make me Manhattans when I was young, so they remind me of him. He was an electrical engineer with AT&T when people still had landline phones in their houses. He was Scottish, reserved, but also very funny. And he was wise. He taught me the most important lesson of my life, which was: "Mary Louise, it's not so much the decisions you make in life that count—it's what you do after you make those decisions that really matters." I remembered that whenever I thought of leaving George. Every marriage goes through difficult periods and I had to figure out how to get through this one.

I took my first sip of the Manhattan. It was just right. Just sweet enough.

"This is perfect, Peter," I said. I sank into the red- and cream-colored cushions of the couch against one wall of our living room. The whole room was red and cream, with a smaller couch like the one I was sitting on under the wide window looking out on our front lawn. Two dark red velvety armchairs were across the room against the wall. Now that the children were grown, I had indulged myself in a pure white wall-to-wall rug. The bar was a deep rosewood matching the sides and back of the couches. I put my Manhattan down on the large glass-topped table in front of the two couches. It was a completely soul-satisfying room that made me feel good whenever I walked into it.

I was totally relaxed and mellow after a few sips of the Manhattan when the front door opened and George strode into the living room, a frown on his face.

"Peter, would you mind moving your giant van out of my driveway. I can't put my car away," he said. No *hello* or *Nice to see you guys* or *How are you, honey?* Just his usual growl.

Peter jumped up. "Sorry about that, George. I'll move it." He left, and Tina, my warm and gracious friend, gave George a kiss on the cheek.

"How nice to see you again, George," she said. "How are you?"

"I'd be a lot better if I didn't come home after working all day to find my driveway blocked," he said, going straight to the bar and filling a glass with Scotch and soda.

"Honey," I said, trying to change the whole mood of doom and gloom descending on us, "Peter and Tina are staying for dinner. Peter drove us into and out of the city. I knew you'd be glad to see them."

He scowled and didn't say anything. He took a big gulp of his drink and threw his coat on the chair.

Peter came back in, took one look at George's face, and realized he was in no mood for dinner guests.

"Maybe we'd better take a rain check on that dinner, Weezie," he said. "George looks like he could use a little peace and quiet. I know that feeling."

Tina picked up his cue.

"Peter's right, hon," she said to me. "Let's do this another time."

I tried to protest, but she was already pulling on her coat and nudging Peter toward the door.

"See you tomorrow, Weezie," she said to me, and I nodded, tears in my eyes. She hugged me and whispered in my ear, "It's all right, sweetie."

When they were gone, I glared at George, who was pouring himself another Scotch.

"Could you have been any ruder?" I asked. "What's the matter with you? They're good friends."

"I've had a rough day," he said. "Leave me alone, Mary Louise. You shouldn't have invited people for dinner without telling me. I don't feel like talking to anybody." He put his head in his hands.

I went over to him and put my arm around his shoulders.

"I'm sorry," I said. "What happened?"

"You wouldn't understand," he said impatiently. "One of my lawyers quit because I wouldn't make him a partner. I lost one of my cases I've been working on for months. Another client wants to go to trial, but there's no room in the court schedule. Nothing went right."

"I'll fix you some dinner," I said. "Salmon and anchovies—okay?"

"I don't care," he said. "Whatever."

I went into the kitchen, my happy mood gone, the promise of a lovely dinner party finished, my need for Mike intensified.

George and I shared a miserable dinner, barely speaking. I went to bed early and was asleep by the time he turned in.

RECIPE FOR SALMON AND ANCHOVIES

Serves 4

3 T. softened butter
4 minced anchovy fillets, with the skin on
2 garlic cloves minced
4 salmon fillets
2 T. capers
Salt and pepper to taste
Half a lemon

1. Preheat oven to 400 degrees.
2. Add the minced anchovies, garlic, salt, and pepper to the softened butter.
3. Melt half the butter mixture in a large oven-proof pan.
4. Brown the skin side of the salmon for three minutes. Baste with butter from the pan while it's cooking.
5. Add capers.
6. Put salmon in the oven for 10 minutes.
7. Take the salmon out of the pan and keep it warm while you add the rest of the anchovy butter to the pan and melt it.
8. When the butter is melted, pour it over the salmon and squeeze the lemon over the buttery salmon.

Fast and easy and so good!

Mary Louise's cooking tip: If you don't feel like making the crabcakes in this chapter, go to a nice restaurant with your best friend and order them there.

Chapter 3

Scoop It!

The next morning was just as silent. I counted the minutes until I heard Peter's car in the drive, and left George with a kiss on the cheek and a "Not sure when I'll be home—I'll call you."

He didn't even answer me.

Tina got out of the car when I came out of the house and put her arm around me to guide me into the van. "You okay?" she asked in a low voice.

"I will be when I get away from here," I said. "Tina I'm so sorry about—"

"Forget it, hon," she said, interrupting me. "We understood. We've all been through it. Don't worry. Help yourself to croissants and coffee."

Peter turned and smiled as I got into the car. "Have some coffee, beautiful."

"Peter, I'm so—"

"Don't give it a second thought," he said, reaching over the seat to squeeze my hand. "I love you anyway."

Janice, Gini, and Pat were already in the van, and they all reached over to give me a hug or a pat on the arm. I was so grateful to these good friends who helped me through everything.

"Got your tap shoes, Weez?" Tina asked, handing me a cup of hot coffee and a croissant.

"Right here in my bag," I said.

"We're off," Peter said, and steered the car out of the driveway and toward the highway.

In less than an hour, we were piling out of the car in front of Radio City. "Have fun, guys," Peter said. "Try not to get anyone else killed."

Tina hit him on the head and joined us on the sidewalk. "See you later, ghoul," she said to him.

Marlowe was waiting for us on the stage. Again, no smile on her face. Just a look that said *I really don't want to bother with these amateurs, but we signed a contract with them so I have to put up with them.*

"Let's get started," she said. "These three will show you how to do the dance and put you through the exercise workouts." She pointed to the three women standing near her.

The first was the dancer who wore the silver earrings the day before. She was holding Ranger, the cat mascot, who snuggled up to her as she said hello to us.

"Hi, Hoofers. I'm Nevaeh Anderson, and I'll show you the routine. It looks simple, but it takes a lot of work to make it seem that easy. Are you ready for some really vigorous rehearsals?"

"We're ready," Gini said. "Just show us what to do."

Pat reached over and patted Ranger, who bumped her nose against her hand. I'm really a dog person, but this cat had already won me over. She was so sweet and approachable. I patted her too.

"Could I hold her?" Pat asked. She's the real cat lover in our group. She even fell in love with a kitten in Brazil and was going back to get her when she was older.

"Of course," Nevaeh said. She put a couple of cat treats in Pat's hand. "Give her these. She'll be your friend for life. They taste like chicken, they tell me."

Ranger nibbled up the little treats and licked her lips. "Meow," she said and jumped on the floor to lap up some of the water in her bowl on the side of the stage away from the dancers.

"We know how hard you Rockettes work," Tina said. "We're here to knock ourselves out. Put us to work."

Nevaeh smiled. "Yell if you need a rest," she

said. "Sometimes we forget how tough this can be."

Another Rockette stepped forward and held out her hand. "I'm Danielle Jennings," she said. "Welcome. I know it's hard, but once you get into it, it's really fun. It's dancing, after all. I'll help you with the exercises that will limber you up so the routine will be easier."

She was about five feet, six inches tall, had brown hair, a smiley face, and a body that seemed a little rounder than the other Rockettes'. That surprised me because they were all so rail-thin I wondered if they ever ate anything but lettuce leaves.

Tina shook her hand and said, "We really need the exercise, Danielle. We've never done such exacting dancing before. Usually we just fling ourselves about, and it's different every time. We have a lot to learn."

"Don't worry," another Rockette said, moving in closer. She was also beautiful, with blond-streaked brown hair and cheekbones to die for. "We'll show you how and work with you until you get it right. I'm Andrea Shapiro. I'll help you work around your Santa outfits. Sometimes they get in the way because of that blasted stomach, but I can show you a few tricks to avoid that."

"I think Glenna said something about getting rid of those stomachs so the costumes wouldn't be so heavy," Tina said.

"Glenna's not here anymore," Marlowe said. "And if we have to dance in forty-pound costumes, so do you."

"Cool it Marlowe," Andrea said. "We'd all be better off without that extra weight."

"As I said, Andrea," Marlowe said. "I'm in charge now. I decide whether to keep them the way they've been or change them. Got that?"

"Got it," Andrea said. From the resentful expression on her face, I gathered she wasn't crazy about Marlowe either.

There was silence for a minute and then Gini spoke up. I held my breath. I could see a little problem here between Marlowe and our outspoken Gini.

"We'll do whatever we have to do," Gini said, "including wearing these jackets." She paused and then asked, "Is there any news about what happened to Glenna?" When there was no answer, just nervous glances among the Rockettes, Gini said, "Are we just going to ignore the fact that she's dead and rehearse as if nothing happened? I mean, she fell into the wheels under the stage. How could that happen?"

Marlowe's stare at Gini was so icy we could feel the chill all over the huge stage. "Of course we're devastated that Glenna is no longer here," she said. "She was our leader, after all. But we have work to do. The Christmas show takes every ounce of concentration and physical strength we have."

She moved closer to Gini. "What's your name?" she said, her tone unfriendly, almost menacing.

"Gini Miller," our fiercest hoofer said, standing her ground, not backing away.

"We are crushed that she's not with us anymore, of course, Ms. Miller," Marlowe said. "But the fact is, the show will open in a month and we have a lot of work to do to get ready for it. People expect the Rockettes to be perfect, and you can either work as hard as we do or leave. I never understood why we needed another group to dance with us anyway."

Tina spoke up immediately. "Marlowe," she said in a conciliatory tone, "we love being part of the Rockettes and are thrilled that Glenna asked us to be in your show. We appreciate the fact that you're keeping us on. I promise we'll work hard not to disgrace you. We'll add a little something different to the Christmas show. A little humor. I think you'll be pleased."

Marlowe relaxed a little. She almost smiled. The Tina charm worked its usual magic. "Well, I hope you know what you're getting yourselves into," she said. She turned her back on us and spoke to the three Rockettes who would be helping us. "They're all yours, guys. Do your best."

With that, she left the stage and our three teachers all talked at once, trying to reassure us that it wasn't that bad, that we could do it, that Marlowe was a little uptight.

"A little uptight!" Gini said. "She'll burst if she gets any more rigid. Is she always like that or does she just dislike us?"

"It's not you Hoofers, Gini," Andrea said. "She's against anything Glenna set up. We've never had any outsiders in our shows before, and Marlowe doesn't like changes in our routine."

"We want to be as good as you are," Gini said. "Just show us what to do and we'll do it."

"Let us show you the Santa routine," Nevaeh said, "and then we'll teach it to you step by step. Okay?"

"Sounds good," Tina said.

Andrea switched on the music. The three Rockettes stood one in back of the other, step-step-kicking in a slower, more lumbering fashion than they usually danced. They held a bell in each hand and jingled them in time to the music raising them over their heads, then bending over and ringing them, then standing up, moving in unison, kicking but not as high as they normally did. I could see why we were chosen to do the Santa Claus part. It was slower, a little easier.

Gini noticed too. "How come you moved more slowly than you usually do?" she asked.

"It's because we'll be wearing these darn forty-pound Santa costumes we told you about," Andrea said. "We look and dance like fat Santa Clauses. Our faces—yours too—will be covered with white beards and we have these stomachs sticking out that definitely slow us down."

"But it works," Nevaeh said. "We have eight numbers in each show and most of them are our regular fast, high-stepping Rockettes deal in minimal costumes. But this one is a change of pace that the audience always loves. They cheer and clap for this number more than any of the others."

"Is that why Glenna asked us to be in this part of the show?" Gini asked. "Because it's not as demanding as the other dances?"

"I don't really know if that's what she had in

mind," Nevaeh said tactfully, "but it kind of makes sense, don't you think? No reflection on you guys, but it's taken us years to perfect all our dances in this Christmas show. I think you'll be glad yours is a little slower."

"You're probably right," Gini said. "Will we get a chance to rehearse in the costumes?"

"Definitely," Danielle said. "Those costumes are really difficult to dance in, so you'll get plenty of practice."

"I don't know about the rest of you," Pat said, "but I'm glad we have a slower dance. I was worried about keeping up with you. You're so fast . . ."

"And so perfect!" Janice said. "This way, if we make a mistake, it will just be part of the Santa Claus fat act."

"Don't think you can make a mistake," Andrea said sharply. "You have to be perfect too. Slower but not sloppy. Can you do that?"

"Of course we can," Tina said. "Let's not waste any more time talking about it. Show us what we have to do."

"Well, first," Danielle said, "you have to do some exercises to limber up a little. Unless you've been dancing every day like we have, you have to get your muscles in shape. Did I mention you have to wear heels when you dance? Also when you rehearse, so you get used to them. You don't have to wear them today, but starting tomorrow—heels and your Santa jacket."

Gini groaned. "You're kidding! A fat suit and heels. How do you do it?"

"It gets easier after a while," Danielle said,

giving us an encouraging smile. I liked her a lot. She seemed to want to help us.

"Did you bring workout clothes with you?" Andrea asked.

"We're wearing them," Tina said.

We all stripped down to leotards and leggings under our tops and jeans. I was glad we had them because this sounded like it was going to be one long, sweaty day.

And it was. Danielle started us off with head rolls, shoulder rolls, arm swings, and side bends. *This isn't so bad,* I thought. *I can do this.*

I was really getting into the side bends when Danielle had us move our whole bodies around and around. Sort of a circular, all-encompassing side bend. Knee hugs were next, followed by slide lunges and calf stretches.

"Okay," she said. "I've been easy on you so far."

We all groaned. "That's your idea of easy?" Gini said.

"Compared to this next move," Nevaeh said. "Now I want to show you our scoop. It's to stretch your hamstrings. You'll feel it when you get home tonight, but it's the most valuable of all our exercises. Here's what you do: Put your weight on your back leg and stretch the other leg up off the floor. Then reach toward that foot that's up in the air and scoop your arms toward you like you're scooping up a whole bowl of ice cream. Then you switch legs and do it again. Got it? Let's see you try it."

I was wobbly at first, but after a few scoops, it

was better. I could see that this Rocketting was going to take a lot of grunting and groaning before we were through. I wished she hadn't mentioned ice cream, though, because I could have used a large dish of chocolate fudge chunk.

After the scooping, we did push-ups and leg raises and running in place. Then we did some backward jogging. Don't ask. We worked out on a treadmill, on an exercise bike, and did sit-ups. By the time Danielle finished with us after an hour, we were panting and praying for a rest.

Finally, she stopped, mopped her neck with a towel, and smiled.

"Okay, you guys," she said. "go take a shower, grab some lunch, and be back here at two o'clock."

I was so relieved to hear that there was some place we could shower and that I would have time for lunch with Mike that I almost hugged her. I called Mike on my cell and asked him if he was free.

"Of course," he said. "Meet me at Bryant Park Grill as soon as you can get there."

I showered and dressed in record time and ran over to the restaurant on Fortieth Street between Fifth and Sixth Avenues. The Christmas gift booths were being set up around the park in front of the restaurant. When I walked in, the stunning woman behind the entrance desk smiled when she heard I was meeting Mike and led me to a table by a window where he was waiting.

"Thanks, Houri," he said to her. He kissed me before I sat down.

"You're all rosy," he said. "You look beautiful."

"It's a wonder I'm not bright red," I said. "Mike, I've never worked so hard in my life. By the time we finish this job I'll have lost twenty pounds."

"Then eat up," he said. "I love you just the way you are."

"What's good here?" I asked.

"Everything," he said. "Try the Caesar salad with chicken. It's really good. Or the crabcakes. They have a great smoked-salmon scramble with asparagus, caviar, and brioche. Or there's a wild-mushroom ravioli you'll never forget."

I ordered the crabcakes from a friendly waiter who shook hands with Mike and said, "Good to see you again, Doc."

"You too, Doc," Mike said, and then explained to me after he left: "His initials are MD so I call him 'Doc'. He's a really good guy."

That was so Mike. It was wonderful to be with him. To be with someone who liked me—loved me, in fact—and wanted to be with me and didn't get mad at me for anything. He made friends everywhere he went.

"So what's it like, being a Rockette?" he asked

"Hard work, but fun," I said. "It's just—oh, Mike—it's just that I never thought in a million years that I'd be dancing with the Rockettes, in Radio City Music Hall, in New York, in their Christmas show. After all those years of sitting out front and marveling at their precision, their perfection, their incredible dancing. And now, for just a little while, I'll be one of them. Who would have thought?"

"If anyone could be a Rockette, it's you," he said. "Mary Louise, you can do anything."

I looked at this man, this handsome, kind, loving man who thought I could do anything and wished once again that I could spend the rest of my life with him instead of grouchy old George who found fault with everything I did.

The waiter brought our lunches. My crab-cakes were so good I waved to the waiter to come to our table.

"Do you think you could get me the recipe for this salad, Doc?" I said. "It's so good."

"Of course," he said and went back to the kitchen to get the information I wanted.

We talked for an hour about my dancing, the twins he delivered in the middle of the night, about New York and all the things we should see since I would be there every day, about my children and his children and my Hoofer friends.

"Since you're such a big carousel fan," he said, "We have to go down to the new one in Battery Park."

"What's it like?" I said, always ready to add a new carousel to my collection.

"It's unbelievable," Mike said. "There's a whole bunch of fish going up and down and around and around in what looks like a glass fish tank. You ride on a seat in the middle of the fish for about three or four minutes and this great music plays—Mozart, Prokofiev, beautiful. You'd love it."

"And so would David," I exclaimed. "I can't wait to tell Pat about this. We could take him

there the next time he's in town. Can two people fit into one fish?"

"A grownup and a little child can fit. David
would probably have his own fish."

"Pat would have the best time. She loves
David so much. He's like her own child."

There was still some time left before I had to
go back to the theater, and I knew what I
wanted to do. Mike's talk about the fish carousel
reminded me of a merry-go-round I loved, one
very close by.

"Mike," I said and stopped, embarrassed.

"What is it?" he asked, leaning forward and
putting his hand on mine.

"One of the reasons I love this restaurant," I
said, "is because there's a carousel in the park."

"I've seen it," he said. When I didn't say anything else, he looked at me. "And you want to
go on it, right?"

"I do, but if you don't mind, I want to go on it
by myself," I said. "I don't know why. I just do."

"I understand," he said. And I knew, being
Mike, he did. "Come on. I'll walk you over there,
and then I'll go back to the hospital."

He paid for our meal. When the waiter came
to pick up the check, he gave me the recipe for
crabcakes. I thanked him and said goodbye to
Houri. Mike and I walked the short distance to
the merry-go-round I loved in Bryant Park. We
threaded our way through the little tables and
chairs in the park, through people working on a
computer or talking to a friend or eating a slice

of pizza until I got to my favorite carousel, just about to start on its next ring-around.

I don't tell everybody this. Just certain tuned-in-to-life people. I find a merry-go-round everywhere I go and ride on it. I sort of collect them. When I climb up on one of those horses and the funky organ music starts to play and the carousel starts its joyful round, I'm back in my childhood.

There was one near us when I was ten that had brass rings to reach for. I thought of them as gold rings. That's kind of my philosophy of life: Always reach for the gold ring. When I was a child and managed to grab one, I got a free ride as a reward. It was hard to actually grab that ring because the carousel flew by so fast, so it was all the more an accomplishment. I always felt I had earned that free ride.

My life, especially since I started dancing with my friends, has had lots of gold rings. Trips to Russia and Spain, to Paris and Rio, to say nothing of the deepening friendship with these incredible women. No brass rings any more in most carousels, including this one, but I didn't care. I could pretend I caught one.

I bought my ticket from Mildred, who knew my name because I had been there so often. I climbed up on my favorite horse, a gold and white steed, lovingly hand-painted like the rest of the horses on this carousel. I had given him the name Blythe Spirit. There were only a few other people riding with me, all of them children with their mothers. I held onto the pole in the middle of my horse, and soon the music started. It was Edith Piaf singing "Padam, Padam,

Padam." Perfect. Just like the one in the Tuileries in Paris when we were there dancing on the *Bateau Mouche.*

The horse rose up and went down. The carousel turned, and I could see Bryant Park, the little statue of Goethe, the office buildings around the park, the people walking by who weren't the least bit surprised to see a woman in her fifties riding a merry-go-round in the middle of the day. It was New York. One of my favorite things about that city is that you can do just about anything you want as long as you don't kill anyone. Nobody really reacts very much. They're all doing their own thing, and it's fine with them if you want to do yours.

The ride was only about five minutes long. I reveled in every second of it. I was no longer a wife and mother and responsible adult. I was that little girl again, riding a magic horse, reaching for the gold ring.

When the ride was over, when the music had stopped, when my childhood was over, I climbed down, patted Blythe Spirit on the nose, and went back to the theater.

RECIPE FOR CRABCAKES

Serves eight light eaters or four very greedy people.

1 lb. fresh crabmeat
½ cup red bell pepper, chopped
½ cup chopped shallots
3 T. chopped fresh basil or 1 tsp. dried basil
2 T. fresh lemon juice
2 T. mayonnaise
1 T. Dijon mustard
½ tsp. Tabasco sauce
dash Worcestershire sauce
3¼ cups fresh bread crumbs
1 large egg
2 T. salted butter
2 T. vegetable oil
tomato salsa

1. Mix first nine ingredients in a large bowl. Add salt and pepper.
2. Add ¼ cup of the breadcrumbs and the egg. Mix thoroughly into the other ingredients.
3. Shape the mixture into eight patties.
4. Coat patties with the rest of the breadcrumbs.
5. Cook the patties in the butter and vegetable oil until they're golden brown on each side.
6. Serve with tomato salsa.

Mary Louise's cooking tip: Luckily none of the things Alice ate in Wonderland made her fatter—just taller. Nothing wrong with that.

Chapter 4

I'm Late, I'm Late For A Very Important Date

I was ready to start dancing, but Detective Carver was back on stage, waiting for the rest of the Rockettes to join us. When everyone had assembled, he spoke to us.

"I'm afraid I must delay your rehearsal for a little while. I apologize, but we have some new information about Glenna Parson's death. I would like to speak to Marlowe Stanley, Nevaeh Anderson, Danielle Jennings, Andrea Shapiro and Shelli Anderson in one of the dressing rooms, please. The rest of you may either wait here or leave."

Our three teachers and Shelli and Marlowe followed the detective offstage.

"Now what?" Janice asked.

"I guess we just wait until he finishes with them," Tina said.

Just then, one of the Rockettes ran onto the stage.

"Are you Tina?" she asked

"I am," Tina answered.

"Well, Marlowe asked me to give you a message," she said. "She told me to tell you that you can leave now because it doesn't look like there will be time for any more rehearsals today."

"Thanks," Tina said, then turned to us. "That's it, gang. We might as well have another New York day and come back tomorrow. Do whatever you want and meet me here at five. Either Peter will take us home or I'll hire a car. I'm going back to the Frick to make more reception plans if anyone wants to come along."

That sounded good to me. I hadn't been to the Frick for a while. It was my favorite museum in New York. "I'm coming with you, Tina."

The others got out their phones to contact their friends, and Tina and I left to get a cab.

The minute we stepped in the door of that venerable museum on Seventy-First Street and Fifth Avenue, I felt as if I were in the home of an old, very rich friend. Tina took my hand and led me into the garden court in the center of the main floor.

"We can't actually have the wedding in the museum—they don't allow that. But we can have the reception here. It will be in this garden," she said, her voice hushed.

I could not think of a lovelier place to have a reception. An oval pool surrounded by roses and oleanders graced the center of the court, with little cupids tucked under the flowers and a large fountain in the middle the focal point of the garden. A nude statue watched over one side of the room, a winged angel the other. Pairs of majestic Ionic columns framed the room on three sides. The arched skylight above brightened the room. We were the only people in the garden court on this day. Its serenity embraced me.

"Oh, Tina, this is exquisite," I said, sitting down on one of the white marble benches beside the pool.

"Isn't it?" she said, joining me. "I needed to find the perfect place because I've been putting this wedding off for such a long time. I love Peter, but I couldn't shake off the feeling that I was somehow being disloyal to Bill to get married again. We had such a good marriage, Weezie."

"I remember," I said. Bill was a wonderful husband and he adored Tina.

"Peter has been an angel," Tina said. "He doesn't push me, but I know how much he wants to get married. A couple of months ago—right after we got back from Rio—he brought me here. He didn't say anything, but when I saw this garden and the rooms with the paintings, rooms with furniture in them just the way they were when the Fricks lived in them, I knew I wanted to have my reception in this garden. I kissed Peter on this bench and told him I would plan the wedding right away if we could have the reception in the museum. I'm sure that's why he brought me here. He just hugged me and said, 'Of course, darling.'"

"It's perfect," I said. We inhaled the peace and silence of this lovely garden for a few minutes, and then Tina stood up and said, "Come see the Living Hall. It's my favorite."

I followed her into the Living Hall, which was a large oak-paneled room, upon which some of the most impressive paintings in the world hung. Bellini's enormous *St. Francis in the Desert* dominated the room. On one side of it, Titian's thoughtful, dreamy *Portrait of a Man in the Red Cap* contrasted with his *Pietro Aretino*, which portrays a powerful man aware of his own exalted place in the society of his time. Holbein's *Sir Thomas More* glared across the room at More's mortal enemy *Thomas Cromwell*, also painted by Holbein. Paintings by Reynolds and Gainsborough lined the walls on both sides of the room.

"There are three Vermeers in this museum," Tina said. "There's only about thirty-six paintings by him in the whole world. Janice will be thrilled that we're having the reception here. She loves Vermeer more than anyone I know. I understand how she feels. He's one of my favorites too."

She pulled me over to Vermeer's *Mistress and Her Maid*.

"I love this painting," she said. "I made up a whole story to go with it. The maid is handing her mistress a note from her lover. She's married to a rich Dutch merchant, but she's bored and is having an affair with her music teacher. The light from the window shines down on her velvet gown with the ermine trim. There are pearls woven into her hair in back. And because of Tracy Chevalier's book, *Girl with a Pearl Earring*, I believe the maid is the model for that painting."

"Me too," a voice in back of us said. We turned around and saw Rockette Andrea Shapiro standing there.

"Hi, you two," she said. "The police questioned me first, so I ran over here to help you plan your reception. I work at this museum the rest of the year when I'm not dancing at the Music Hall."

"Fantastic," Tina said. "What do you do here?"

"I arrange events in the museum, especially wedding receptions. I love doing this. Glenna didn't want me to have two jobs. She wanted me to work with her at Radio City planning events for the Rockettes in other cities. I didn't want to do that, and I told her so, but she kept dredging up stuff for me to do so I couldn't come here. Now I'm free to spend all the time I want at the Frick. Marlowe is fine with it."

She saw the look Tina and I exchanged and added hastily, "Not that I'm glad Glenna is dead, of course. I just meant, it's easier now. Come on in my office, and we can plan the food and the music and everything else we need to make this the best reception ever."

Tina started to follow her and then remembered I was there. "Oh, Weezie," she said, "Do you want to join us?"

"No, no," I said. "I'll just wander around the museum for a while and then roam around the park before I head back to the theater. I might take the train back home. If I decide to do that, I'll call you and tell you not to wait for me."

"Sounds good," Tina said, following Andrea into another part of the museum.

I strolled around the rooms and corridors of this wonderful old house, enjoying the lightness and change of mood in the Fragonard Room, where the walls are graced with a series of his paintings called *The Progress of Love*. I lingered in the West Gallery to look at landscapes by Constable and Corot and portraits by Rembrandt and Velasquez.

But it was in the South Hall, tucked away in the alcove under the stairs, that I found a painting by my favorite artist, Renoir. It's called *La Promenade*, and it's full of sunshine and color, as all of his paintings are. It's why I love the Impressionists. They always make me feel good, light-hearted. I lingered in front of this scene of a young mother, dressed in dark blue, wearing a lacy, flowery hat, walking along a path with her two little girls, identically clad in turquoise dresses and jackets, trimmed with white fur. One of her daughters is carrying a white fur muff, the other a doll, dressed as elaborately as she is. Both children wear white hats, white tights, and white shoes. There is white lace around the hems of their dresses. The path is lined with flowers and shrubs, and other mothers and fathers and children can be seen in the background.

I think one of the reasons I love Renoir's paintings so much is there was a print of one of his paintings, *Portrait of Madame Georges Charpentier and her Children,* hanging over the fireplace in the living room of my writing professor in college. The seminar she held for six of us who wanted to be writers was held in this room instead of a classroom.

Every week we would submit our stories to her and discuss them, watched over by Madame Charpentier. I can still close my eyes and see that painting. A young mother in a black dress looking lovingly at her two little children in blue dresses trimmed with lace. Both have curly blond hair. One child is sitting on a colorful couch, the other is perched on the back of a sleeping Saint Bernard. There are flowers on a table nearby. A tapestry screen forms a background to the whole lovely scene.

Those seminars were my favorite of all my classes. I gave up writing after college because I needed to make a living, but I wouldn't have missed those afternoons beside that fireplace, watched over by Madame Charpentier, for anything.

When I had had enough of paintings and sculptures, Italian bronzes, Chinese porcelains, and Limoges enamels, I left the Frick and went outside to walk through Central Park. It was a perfect day for it. The weather was crisp and cool. I always feel calm and yet stimulated at the same time in this beautiful park designed by

Frederick Olmsted and Calvert Vaux in 1858. They somehow made the park a combination of action and peace and quiet.

There were lots of places where you could just sit and do nothing, watching other people passing by and making up stories about them. Or you could sit by the pond and watch children sailing boats. You could eat in The Boathouse on the lake, the way Mike and I did the day before. Or, if you had more energy, you could go for a run on the paths set aside for joggers. You could probably also get mugged if you were in the wrong place at the wrong time, but somehow I was never afraid in this park.

As I walked along the path heading north, I saw one of my favorite things in the whole park. The statue of Alice in Wonderland by a little pond. Alice, hair ribbon neatly in place, was sitting on a large mushroom, accompanied by the White Rabbit on the left looking at his watch. I knew he was saying, "I'm late, I'm late, for a very important date," since I read and reread *Alice's Adventures in Wonderland* by Lewis Carroll when I was a child. I even remembered that Lewis Carroll's real name was Charles L. Dodgson.

The Mad Hatter was on Alice's right, looking wildly around for a way to escape. The Cheshire Cat sits on her lap and the March Hare is settled in next to her. I loved this statue. I used to bring James here when he was little. I would lift him up onto the huge mushroom to climb all over Alice and her tea party friends. He never wanted to leave. Neither did I for that matter.

When James and I came here, there were usually lots of other children piling onto the statue too, clinging to Alice's head and to the White Rabbit. I stood in front of the mushroom to catch James if he should slip and fall because it was a long way up for a three-year-old. But he was as sure-footed then as he now was sure of what he wanted to do with his life. He was in law school to become an attorney like his father. He and George were very close. It warmed me to see them together, talking, exchanging stories and memories, loving each other. George was a good father, even if he wasn't all that great a husband lately.

Today, though, I remembered James as a little boy, laughing and tumbling about on Alice's lap with the other children, happy and safe and loved. Lucky child to know without any doubt that he was totally and unreservedly loved by his parents, no matter what mistakes he made or whatever happened to him in life.

When my little boy was ready to leave Alice, we would sit on a bench by the pond and eat the sandwiches I brought with me. Peanut butter and jelly for both of us, with snickerdoodle cookies for dessert. My mother used to make those cookies for me and my sister when I was little, and I made them for my children. I cherish that recipe, smudged and faded.

Those days were so precious. I treasured them at the time. I never took them for granted. I was glad we moved to the suburbs after we had our second son, Sam, but I missed my days with James and Alice and those peanut-butter-and-jelly sandwiches. I missed New York, too, so I

was glad we would have this time in the city
dancing at Radio City.

There were no children around today, so I sat
down on the mushroom next to Alice to bring
back that feeling I had when I was there with
James. I closed my eyes and reveled in the sweet-
ness of those bygone days.

"You look as if you're in Wonderland with
Alice," a familiar voice said. "No, don't get up.
You belong there."

I opened my eyes. Mike was standing there.

"How did you know I was here?" I asked.

"You didn't answer your phone, so I called
Tina and she said you were probably in the park.
I wanted to find out what the detective said. Are
you okay?"

He came over and lifted me down from the
mushroom and my trip back to my young moth-
erhood days. He kissed me. "You looked so
beautiful up there. Come and live with me in my
Wonderland. I'll make you happy. I promise."

I leaned against him. How I wanted to go and
live with him, this strong, kind, funny, loving
man!

"What did the detective tell you?" he asked me.

"Nothing really. He just wanted to question
some of the Rockettes, but he let us go."

"And you ended up here with Alice on her
mushroom."

"Yes. I went to the Frick with Tina first. That's
one of my favorite places in New York, and she's
going to have her wedding reception there."

"Good idea," he said, his hand smoothing my

hair. I didn't want to leave him, but I knew I had to.

"It's time for me to leave Wonderland, Mike," I said. "Time for me to go home."

"All right, Alice," he said. "Are you going back to the theater to ride home with Peter?"

"No, it's a little early for Peter," I said. "I'll take a train home from Penn Station. Can you hail a cab for me please?"

"I have a better way to get you to Penn Station," he said. "You can take a cab any time."

He raised his hand and waved to a man standing next to a horse and carriage nearby. The man climbed into the driver's seat and pulled on the reins to get the horse moving toward us. The horse was white with red flowers around his harness. The cab was dark red with velvety white seats.

"Oh Mike, I've always wanted to ride in one of these, but in all my trips to New York I've never done it. How lovely!"

The driver was in his sixties. He wore a red top hat and a black leather jacket to match his carriage. He jumped down to help me into my seat. Mike got in beside me.

"I thought you'd like this," he said. "Jenny used to love it. Whenever we went to the theater, I would get one of these carriages to bring us back to our apartment after the play."

He touched my face. "And you're so like her, Mary Louise."

The driver got back on his seat and made a "Giddyap"noise to his horse, who started slowly walking along a path going west in the park.

The leaves on the trees in the park were just beginning to turn red and gold. Joggers ran past us, intent on their run. Central Park was at its finest that day. I relaxed and leaned back to enjoy this magical ride through flowers and greenery in the middle of a city built of steel and granite.

Mike put his arm around me and pointed out things to me as we wound slowly west.

"That's one of my favorite fountains in the park," he said, asking the driver to stop for a moment. "It's Bethesda Fountain. It always seems so friendly."

And it was. There was an angel on top of the fountain, birds perched on its wings, little cherubs further down on the fountain, playing in the afternoon sunshine. The clear, cool water sprayed out all around the angel. A few people were seated on benches nearby, playing with their children, watching their babies, reading a magazine or a book, dozing in their chairs. It was a scene of such contentment; I wasn't surprised that it was watched over by an angel.

"He's called *the Angel of the Waters*," Mike said. "A woman named Emma Stebbins sculpted it in 1873." He tapped the driver on the back to let him know we could proceed.

The horse clopped along, not disturbed by the increasing number of cars and cabs passing us as rush hour got closer.

Soon we came to my favorite part of the park, Strawberry Fields. I always loved the Beatles. I took guitar lessons when I was a teenager and my sister and I used to sing their songs enthusiastically. Badly, but enthusiastically. I still remembered that song, "Strawberry Fields Forever," where nothing was real and nothing was too terrible to get hung about. It was a comforting thought for me when I was a teen and never sure everything would turn out all right.

"Could you stop a minute, please, driver?" I asked.

I wanted to look at the memorial for John Lennon, my favorite Beatle because he was so irreverent. I loved the large black-and-white mosaic in the pathway with the word *Imagine* inscribed on it. That song embodied everything I loved about Lennon and Yoko Ono. Their plea for peace and love in a world that seemed to forget that too often. I wanted to join those two dreamers in a peaceful place, where the world could live as one. I'm still waiting for that.

"There are one hundred and sixty-one plants around this memorial," Mike said, "Each one from a different country."

"I used to come here all the time after John was killed," I said. "There was something so comforting about it. It seemed such a fitting memorial to John Lennon."

"My favorite Beatle was George Harrison," Mike said. "He seemed the sanest of those wild four."

"Paul McCartney was the cutest," I said. "I was torn between him and John."

"Ringo was my favorite," the driver said, turning around to talk to us. "He didn't say much. Just made a lot of noise. I like that. People talk too much these days. They're even thinking about getting rid of these horses—some animal rights nuts. They think it's cruel to hitch them to carriages to drive people around. My Daisy loves doing this. I take really good care of her."

"New York without these horses and carriages would lose part of its character, part of what makes New York New York," I said. "This is my first carriage ride, but I always loved seeing all of you lined up outside the park across from the Plaza Hotel."

"You got that right, lady," the driver said. "Ready to go?"

I could have stayed there forever, but I knew I had to get back home and straighten things out with George. I dreaded it, but I knew I had to do it. This carriage ride was a blessing.

"Yes," Mike said. "Take us to Penn Station, please, driver."

RECIPE FOR SNICKERDOODLES

Makes 24 cookies

¼ lb. stick of salted butter, softened
¾ cup sugar
1 egg
1½ cup flour
1 tsp. cream of tartar
1 tsp. baking soda
¼ tsp. salt
3 T. sugar
3 tsp cinnamon

Preheat oven to 375 degrees.
1. Mix the butter, sugar, and egg together.
2. Mix the flour, cream of tartar, baking soda, and salt together, and add to the butter mixture.
3. Chill the mixture until you can make little balls the size of walnuts out of it.
4. Mix the cinnamon and sugar together.
5. Roll the balls in cinnamon and sugar.
6. Butter a flat baking pan.
7. Bake cookies for about six minutes. Cookies should be crispy but not hard.

Mary Louise's cooking tip: Veal piccata doesn't always settle a quarrel—but it can't hurt!

Chapter 5

It's A Good Thing I Know How To Cook

I hated having George mad at me. I've always been afraid when people are mad at me since I was a little girl. I never did understand that people got angry sometimes, that it really had nothing to do with me. They were just mad at what was happening to them in their lives, and they spoke angrily to me. I guess children never really know that they didn't do anything bad. They just get caught in the undertow.

By the time I turned the key in the lock of our front door, it was almost time for George to come home. Tucker was there to greet me, his tail wagging.

"Hello, you good old dog," I said, giving him a hug. "Are you ready for your dinner?"

He followed me into the kitchen where I piled some food into his dish.

I checked out the fridge and decided to make veal scallops with pine nuts for our dinner. It was one of George's favorites. I needed to come to some kind of understanding with him so we weren't always mad at each other every time I left the house to dance.

When I heard his key in the door, I came out of the kitchen and put my arms around him.

"Hi honey," I said. "Are you okay?"

"Why wouldn't I be?" he said, already on the defensive.

"George, we have to talk," I said.

"Must we?" he said. "I've been talking all day in court."

"I'm not one of your clients," I said. "I'm your wife. I love you. And you're always mad at me these days."

"You're never here to be mad at," he said, hanging his coat in the closet.

"Do you want me to give up dancing with my friends?" I asked.

"Yes," he said. "But you'll never do it."

"I love dancing, George. Can't you understand that? It gives another dimension to my life. I get to travel all over the world. And moving to music is as natural to me as breathing."

"Mary Louise, I love you. I know you love dancing, but I need you to be here with me when I get home from work. I want to talk to you, laugh with you, tell you what happened to me. I married you because I'd rather be with you than anyone else in the world, and for the last two years you're off in Russia or Spain or Paris or Rio. I miss you."

I looked at his face. He was in pain. I was causing it.

I kissed him and pulled him over to the sofa. "Let's compromise," I said. "If you'll put up with my going off to New York every day to rehearse for this Christmas show—oh, George, we're going to be Santa Clauses, it's hilarious. If you can be okay with that, I promise to be here every night when you get home to make your dinner and talk to you. No late night rehearsals. How does that sound?"

He looked relieved. "That would be great. But what will you do if the others have to stay late to rehearse? You can't just get up and leave."

"I'll make sure they understand that's what I'm going to do, and they can either go on without me or leave too."

He held me close. "I love you so much," he said. "Thanks for working this out. I know what this means to you."

I kissed him. "How about some veal piccata?"

"Sounds wonderful," he said.

I went back into the kitchen and got out the ingredients for the veal dish. I needed to fry some bacon first so I could cook the floured veal briefly in the bacon drippings mixed with a little butter. When the veal was cooked, I took it out of the pan and kept it warm under foil. I added some white wine to the frying pan and scraped up all the yummy pieces left in there and mixed them into the wine. When the wine was reduced, I added some more butter, some pine nuts, capers, sage, and the bacon bits.

Meanwhile I had made some rice and stirred up a salad. I poured the sauce over the veal, served the rice, and took the whole meal to the dining room table. I lit the tall red candles in the center of the table, put some fresh water in the vase with the pink and white carnations, and poured a couple of glasses of Côtes du Rhône red wine.

I called George, and he sat down, raised his glass of wine to me, and said, "To my love."

I started to tell him about Radio City and the police and the Frick, but he wanted to tell me about the case he had tried in court that day, so for the millionth time, I shut up and listened to him. I realized I was looking forward to tomorrow when I could talk to Mike, who listened to me.

RECIPE FOR VEAL PICCATA

Serves 2

4 very thin veal scallops
3 bacon slices
1 c. flour 4 T. butter
½ cup dry white wine (Chardonnay or Chablis are good)
3 T. pine nuts
1 T. capers
½ tsp. dried sage

1. Chop up the bacon slices and fry them until they're crisp. Put them on paper towels.
2. Sprinkle salt and pepper on the veal scallops and dredge them in the flour.
3. Add one tablespoon of the butter to the bacon drippings and cook the veal very quickly on both sides and take them out of the pan. Put some foil over them to keep them warm.
4. Add the wine to the pan and boil it until there's about four tablespoons left.
5. Put the other three tablespoons of butter in the skillet.
6. Add the pine nuts, capers, sage, and bacon bits.
7. Pour the sauce over the veal, and serve to your lucky eating partner.

> **Mary Louise's cooking tip: Croque Madame is pronounced *Croak Madame*, but you don't really have to kill her—maybe just raise her cholesterol a little.**

Chapter 6

And Baby Makes Three

I got into Peter's car the next morning ready to tell my friends about my agreement with George, but they were all talking over each other, comparing notes about the police, the Rockettes who were questioned, and what happened after Tina and I left the theater.

"Bring me up to date," I said. "What happened?"

"We were sitting around calling people and making plans to meet them when Danielle came out of the room where the chief was questioning

her and the other four Rockettes," Janice said.
"We thought she'd leave right away, but she
came over to us and you could tell she wanted to
talk to us.

"So did she tell you anything?" I asked, my
story about George and rehearsals and all that
shoved aside.

"She sure did," Janice said. "Wait till you hear,
Weezie. Tell her, Gini."

Gini handed me a cup of coffee and a muffin
and continued. "She kept saying, 'I shouldn't
talk about this' and looking toward the office. It
was obvious she didn't want the others to know
she was talking to us. But she couldn't help herself. She talked in a really low voice and . . ."

"What did she say?" I asked.

"She was mad that the police were questioning her. She kept saying 'I didn't *do* anything.'
She emphasized the *do*. I felt like she knew what
had happened but wasn't an active participant
in it."

"Active in what?" I said. "What are you talking
about, Gini?"

"Well, she said something like, 'It wasn't my
idea.' "

"What wasn't her idea?" I asked, getting more
and more exasperated.

"We got the distinct impression that she knew
but was afraid to tell us," Pat said. "It was just a feeling, you know? She never actually said, 'I know
what happened to her,' but she looked like she
was about to tell us when the others came out of
the office, and she shut up right away."

"You're making this whole thing up, based on

your feelings," Peter said, driving out onto the main road. "Lawyers are taught from the first minute in law school that you base your case on facts, on what actually happened, not on people's feelings."

"You can't dismiss feelings and instincts, Peter," Pat said. "They can lead to the facts."

"Maybe," he said, stopping for a red light.

"So you have this feeling that one of those Rockettes the police chief questioned killed Glenna?" I asked. "And anyway, who said she was murdered? It might have been an accident."

"Right," Gini said sarcastically. "I don't think the detective would keep coming back to question everyone if Glenna's death was a simple accident. Besides, you should have seen the way Marlowe glared at Danielle when she came out of the office, and Danielle left the stage right away. I did hear Nevaeh say to Marlowe in a low voice, 'Why did he question the five of us and none of the other Rockettes?' Marlowe stared pointedly at us and said, 'We can talk about this later, Nevaeh,' while trying to pull her off the stage."

"What's with that Shelli girl?" Janice asked. "She seems to have some kind of relationship with Marlowe. She didn't say anything, but she kept hovering near Marlowe and left with her at the end."

"I noticed that too," Pat said. "Maybe I'm just overly sensitive to woman-to-woman relationships, but I thought there was something more there than friendship."

"I think she's more of a hanger-on than a

lover," Gini said. "She's the type that always wants to kiss up to the boss. There's one in every crowd."

"I still don't understand what you found out that you didn't know before," I said.

"Me too, kid," Peter said. "Come on, Gini. What else did you find out?"

Gini took a bite of her muffin. "These are really good, Peter," she said. "I love blueberry muffins." She handed one to him and continued. "I don't have any real clues to prove this, you understand, but Detective Carver must have had a good reason to single out those five Rockettes, out of 80 dancers, to question. Oh, I forgot to tell you: Andrea Shapiro, the first one he questioned, left his office before the others because she wanted to go to the Frick and help Tina with her reception plans."

"I was glad to see her," Tina said. "She was a huge help."

"Yeah, but before she left the theater, she came over to us," Gini continued. "And in a low voice, she said, 'Glenna wasn't the perfect, I-love-everybody efficient leader of the Rockettes, you know.' I almost fell over. I wasn't expecting her to say anything bad about Glenna. I said, 'What do you mean?' She started to say something more, but she must have realized she had said too much because she muttered something and left."

"So Glenna wasn't loved by every one of the Rockettes," Peter said. "You need a better motive than that to kill someone, or we'd all be dead."

Good old Peter. He always brought us down to earth.

"I still say all five of those Rockettes are hiding something," Gini said. "You'll see."

When we arrived at the theater, Danielle was the only person waiting for us on the stage. She had a big pile of Santa jackets next to her.

"Hi there, Hoofers," she said. "Come on up here. I thought it would be a good idea for you to rehearse in these jackets today, so you can get used to dancing with this extra weight."

"Good idea, Danielle," Tina said. "I've been wondering what they would feel like."

We all grabbed a jacket, and I almost fell down when I put mine on. There was this giant round ball sewn into the front of the jacket that felt every bit of its forty pounds. How were we supposed to dance in these things?

Gini, of course, was the first to complain.

As she struggled to zip up her jacket, she said, "Danielle, I can't move in this thing. Can't we get rid of the heavy ball that's in here?"

"We've all complained about it," Danielle said. "Believe me, Gini, we all hate these jackets. But the dance just isn't right without them. We move too fast. We're supposed to be fat Santas, dancing in spite of our stomachs. Don't worry. You'll get used to them. We all have."

Gini looked skeptical.

"Let's give it a try, gang," Tina said, putting her arm around Gini. "We can do it."

Danielle turned on the music, and we lined up in back of each other to do the step, step kick, bend, lift, kick of this dance. At first I could barely step, let alone kick, but as we got into it more, I found it a little easier. It would take hours of practice to do this easily, however.

When the music stopped after our fifteen-minute dance, we were all puffing and sweating. We flopped down on the floor, and Danielle applauded us.

"Not bad for the first time, Hoofers," she said. "You'll get there. Don't give up. Now, take the jackets off, and we'll do some leg exercises and push-ups to strengthen your muscles."

We pushed and strained and grunted and groaned for the next couple of hours.

"Go get some lunch," Danielle said. "Be back here at two, and we'll try dancing in the jackets again." She didn't seem to have any inclination to continue her confession of the day before, concerning Glenna's death.

We showered and changed into the clean shirts and pants we had brought with us and separated: Gini off to see Alex; Janice to catch Tom before he went onstage in the matinee of his play: Pat to meet David, who had a week off from school, at the zoo; Tina to the Frick, where she would meet Andrea. I called Mike, who asked me to meet him at Le Bateau Ivre, a small, intimate restaurant in the East Fifties.

He was there, waiting for me. It was very quiet in this small, dark, cozy room. It was a nice enough day so that the windows in the front were open to Fifty-First Street, where there was an occasional sound of cars going by. The couple next to us were speaking in French. Perfect.

"Hi Alice," he said. "How's the dancing going?"

I told him about the Santa jackets. He laughed. "Can't wait to see you in one of those." He took my hand. "I think it's wonderful that you do all these off-the-wall things like dancing in a forty-pound jacket, or sambaing with a member of the audience you've never seen before in Rio, or all the other things that most women don't have the skill or the nerve to do."

It was so good to hear someone actually praise me for doing what I loved to do.

The petite waitress asked if we were ready to order, and I told her I wanted a croque madame.

"What's that?" Mike asked. "I've heard of a croque monsieur but not a croque madame."

"It's just like a croque monsieur only it has a fried egg on top," I said and asked the waitress for an iced tea to go with it.

"What the heck," Mike said. "I'll have one of those too."

When the waitress left, Mike took my hand again and said, "Tell me. What's happening?"

I took a deep breath and dived in. "I had a long talk with George about my dancing last night," I said.

Mike took his hand off mine and took a sip of his water. "What did he say?"

"He said if I have to dance, and he knows I do, would I please be home in time to make him dinner every night, and to be there to talk to him and—"

"And love him," Mike said, the muscles in his face tightening.

"Right," I said.

"And you're going to do that because of the kind of person you are," Mike said. "Which is one of the reasons I love you."

"Oh, Mike," I said, "What am I going to do? I owe him the chance to make our marriage work, but I think all the time how much I want to talk to you. About everything. Especially about what's going on at the theater. I'm in the middle of a murder mystery, and George only wants to talk about elevator shafts."

"I always love talking to you," Mike said. "Who else is surrounded by falling bodies wherever you go? And you're certainly the only one I know who wears everything from a skin-tight black dress to a forty-pound Santa suit when she goes to work."

We both laughed. That's another thing I missed with George. We didn't laugh any more. Everything was so serious and difficult.

My croque madame came, and it was fantastic. I've eaten a lot of croques monsieurs in my life in French restaurants because they are so much more satisfying than regular sandwiches, but I haven't had many croque madames. I didn't feel I needed that fried egg on top of all those other calories, but this one was especially good. Mike was less enthusiastic, but he saw how much I like it and asked the waitress for the recipe, which she brought just as we were finishing our lunches.

"Do you have to go right back?" he asked. "There's some place I want to take you."

I looked at my watch. I still had about forty minutes before I had to be back at the theater.

"If it won't take too long, Mike," I said. "What is it?"

"It's one of my favorite places in the city. Come on, we have to hurry."

He paid the bill, and the waitress gave me the recipe for my croque madame.

Mike found a cab right away and told the driver to take us to Fifty-Third Street between Fifth and Sixth Avenues.

"Stop here, please," Mike said when we came to the entrance to a little park. A sign said it was called Paley Park, named in honor of the father of William Paley, the television executive.

Mike took my hand and led me into this miniature park with a waterfall on one side. It made a soft noise that muffled the other sounds of the city. If you closed your eyes you wouldn't know you were in New York. There were honey locust trees all around the park and ivy climbing up the two walls on either side. A few people were seated in the chairs next to the marble tables. They didn't even look up as we came in. They were reading or eating or just sitting there peacefully enjoying the respite from the noise and fast pace of the city.

Mike took me over to a spot near the waterfall where no one could see us and kissed me.

"I thought this could be our own place when we only had a few minutes to be together," he said. "I could call you and say, 'Meet me in the park,' and we could have a few minutes alone here. It's only a short walk to the Music Hall from here. What do you think?"

"Oh Mike, I think it's a lovely idea." I knew I shouldn't say yes, but it seemed so right. I wanted to stay with him forever. I loved him. I couldn't help it. I loved this good, kind, funny man more than my husband.

We sat down at one of the tables and held hands. The waterfall was the perfect background to my thoughts. We didn't talk, just relaxed into the peace of that moment, our closeness. No matter what happened between us, we would have this to remember later on.

After a while, I looked at my watch and stood up.

"I've got to get back, Mike," I said. "Thank you for this."

"I'll walk you back," he said, and took my hand to lead me out of Paley Park.

When we got back to the theater, he said, "Tomorrow?"

"Probably," I said. "Let's see what happens." I knew I'd see him, no matter what happened.

I ran into the theater, and Pat was the only one on stage. She was struggling to put on her heavy jacket when I joined her.

"These things are impossible," I said.

"They're terrible!" she said.

"How did David like the zoo?" I asked.

"He loved it," she said. "And so did I. I'm so

glad he has the week off from school so I can take him places I love. It's a wonderful zoo. He's such a great kid. We both loved the seals. They clowned for us, diving off rocks into the water, jumping up to be fed. And David liked the polar bears. They swim around and push their noses against the glass. There were snow monkeys in the trees and leopards. I'd forgotten how much fun it is to go to a zoo. David was worried that it was bad for the animals to be confined like that, but after he saw them in this natural environment, he felt better about them."

"He sounds like a wonderful boy," I said. "You and Denise must enjoy him a lot

"We do, Mary Louise," I said. "One of the best things about loving Denise is having her son David in my life. I really think of him as my own.I'm so lucky."

I was silent, distracted. She read my mind. Pat always knows when something is wrong.

"Want to talk about it?" she asked.

"Maybe later when we have more time," I said. "I really need to talk to you, Pat. I'm so confused about Mike."

"I thought so," she said. "I know how much he means to you. I saw you with him in Spain."

"And he means even more now. When we're together, I—"

"Hey there you two," Janice said, jumping up on the stage, interrupting me. She couldn't stop moving. She twirled around the stage, did a couple of cartwheels, hugged me, then sat down next to us, a big smile on her face.

"Okay, Jan," Pat said. "What's happening? You just had lunch with Tom, right?"

"Yes, yes, yes," she said. "And guess what? You'll never guess."

"You're going to marry him," Pat said.

She might as well have punched Janice in the stomach. All the excitement disappeared.

"Oh, Pat, I wanted to tell you," Janice said.

Pat reached over and touched her arm. "I'm sorry, Jan. Forgive me. Forget I said that. Tell us your news."

Janice revved up again just as Tina and Gini joined us on stage. They saw the look on Jan's face, heard Pat ask for her news, and sat down with us.

"Tell us too," Tina said.

"Yeah, Jan, what?" Gini said.

"Tom and I are getting married!" Jan said, so loudly Danielle came running from her office.

"Who's gettting married?" she asked.

Tina filled her in quickly about Tom and Janice's long romance that had lasted through his marriage and a couple of hers and was finally going to end up in their own union.

"Congratulations!" Danielle said. "I hope you'll be as happy as I've been with Phil."

"Is your husband a dancer too?" I asked her.

"No, he's an accountant," she said. She looked around. Then she said, almost in a whisper, "We're going to have a baby. Don't tell anyone, though. No one's supposed to know."

"Why not?" Janice asked.

"Well,"—and again, Danielle looked around—"see, you're not supposed to dance with the

Rockettes if you're pregnant. Glenna told me
when she hired me that if I got pregnant, I'd be
fired. I need this job, so I didn't tell her. Last
week, though, she said something about my gain-
ing weight and that I'd better cut down on calories."

"So how come you're still here?" Gini asked.
"She was bound to find out pretty soon."

"I don't have to worry about that any more,"
Danielle said. "Marlowe's okay with it." She
quickly added, "Not that I'm glad Glenna is
dead. I mean . . . I'm sorry she was . . ." She sort
of fluttered to a stop.

I couldn't help but think there were two
Rockettes who were glad Glenna was dead—Andrea, who wanted to keep working at her outside job at the Frick and still dance with the
Rockettes in the Christmas show, and Danielle,
who also wanted to keep dancing in the show
and keep her baby. Maybe . . . no, that was pre-
posterous. They couldn't be murderers. They
were too nice. If I'd said that to George, he
would have said, "Nobody's too nice to be a
murderer, Mary Louise." I thought of all the ar-
ticles I'd read in the paper about people who
took the lives of several victims, and when the
neighbors were asked about him, they always
said, "He was such a nice young man—so shy
and nice to his mother."

"Tell us more, Janice," Danielle said, chang-
ing the subject. "When are you getting married?"

"When I finish dancing in the Christmas show
with you guys," she said, getting up and twirling

around a couple of times. Janice is just irresistible when she's happy. Beautiful and radiant. We all felt her joy.

"What's happening when you're finished dancing with us?" Nevaeh said coming onto the stage. "Must be something sensational. Can I come too?"

" 'Fraid not, Nevaeh," Jan said, laughing. "I'm getting married."

"Wonderful," she said. "I'm so happy for you."

Marlowe strode onto the stage, her face as stony as always. "Why aren't you rehearsing?" she asked, sobering us all up. "You should be practicing in those Santa jackets. There's no time to sit around chatting."

"Oh, Marlowe," Janice said, "I just got engaged. I'm afraid I'm the one who held us up from rehearsing.

"Congratulations," Marlowe said, still her usual unemotional self. Janice might as well have told her she bought new shoes. "Now, if we can get started with what we're here for. You five have a long way to go before you'll be ready to dance with the Rockettes."

Our ecstatic mood dribbled away. We picked up our dead-weight jackets and struggled into them. Marlowe turned on the music, and "Santa Claus is Coming to Town" blared forth. I was beginning to get sick of that song, sick of these heavy jackets, sick of the whole idea of this show. I could tell by the expressions on my friends' faces, they felt the same way. We usually have fun when we're dancing. It's what we all love

best in the world. We're called the Happy
Hoofers, not the Boo-Hoo Dancers. We still had
another month of rehearsals before the first
show and two more months after that. It was the
first time in my life I didn't want to dance.

But I had to. I put a smile on my face and
dragged my fat-stomached body through the
song.

Marlowe frowned at us. "I know you're all used
to looking happy when you dance," she said. "I
suppose that's why you call yourselves the Happy
Hoofers. Well, you can forget those smiley faces
while you're dancing here. You'll be wearing a
white Santa Claus beard that covers your entire
face, so you can get rid of those phony grins."

Why was this woman so nasty? What had we
ever done to her? I couldn't figure it out. Gini,
of course, came right out and confronted her.

"What's your problem, Marlowe?" she asked.
"You always seem to be mad at us for some reason. Is it something we did, or said, or what?"

Marlowe glared at her. "Well, if you must
know," she said, "I wasn't in favor of hiring you
in the first place. I don't believe in outsiders
dancing with the Rockettes. We're famous for
our perfection, and with all due respect, you're
not exactly perfect. Nowhere near. I have a lot
of problems managing eighty dancers for the
show, and I just don't have time to nurse you
Hoofers through your performance."

"We may not be so great right now," Gini said,
her irritation showing, "but we learn fast. We
work hard, and we can do anything you ask us to

do. This is only our third day, so we could use a little more help from you. And maybe an encouraging word or two, if you can manage that."

"Sorry about that," Marlowe said, not looking at all sorry. "I have too much to do to worry about whether I'm coddling you enough. Just follow Danielle's instructions and you'll be okay." She turned away abruptly and went backstage, where we could see Shelli waiting for her.

Danielle took one look at our downcast expressions and tried to boost our spirits. "You're doing fine, Hoofers," she said. "Don't let Marlowe discourage you. She tends to be—what should I say—uh, on the pessimistic side. Come on, let's try it one more time. Then I'll let you take off those jackets and do some push-ups."

Whoopee! I thought. *Push-ups!* I found it hard to get out of the gloomy spell Marlowe had cast on us.

The music started. We pulled ourselves together, and took our Santas through another time coming to town. I used to love that song.

"Not bad, guys," Danielle said when we finished. "Take off the jackets, and we'll work on your muscles so the forty pounds will be easier to dance with."

She smiled at us and stripped down to her leotard.

She waited until we were all ready and then said, "Okay, one-two- three, push . . . ohhhhhh." She sat up and grabbed her abdomen. Her face was contorted in pain. "Call my doctor," she said to Neveah, who was exercising with us.

Neveah picked up Danielle's phone and speed-dialed her doctor.

"It's Danielle," she said. "She's in trouble. Pains. Yes, doctor, I'll tell her."

"He's sending an ambulance right away, honey," she said to Danielle when she hung up. "Hang in there."

Danielle was doubled over in pain. "I can't lose this baby too," she said. "I lost my last one in the third month. This one means everything to me."

"What hospital is she going to?" I asked Neveah.

"New York Hospital," she said, holding Danielle.

"My friend, Mike Parnell is the head obstetrician there," I said. "I'll call him. He might be able to speed things up."

Danielle nodded. She was in too much pain to speak.

I called Mike, who answered immediately, and told him what was happening.

"I'll clear things here right away, Mary Louise," he said. "Her doctor is excellent. I'll do everything I can to help him."

I told Danielle what he had said, and she groaned a thank-you.

By this time, some of the other Rockettes had come onto the stage. They were all obviously fond of Danielle, and their faces reflected their concern.

"You'll be all right, honey," one of them said to Danielle. "We'll all say a prayer for you."

The ambulance made it across town in fifteen minutes. The medics put Danielle on a stretcher. They worked quickly and efficiently and had her in the van in a few minutes.

"I want to come with you," I said to Danielle. She grabbed my hand and nodded.

"Is that okay with you?" I asked the medics.

"Sure, come on," they said, and I climbed into the back of the van next to Danielle.

"I just can't lose this baby," she said, her voice choked with tears. ". . . ohhhhhh. It hurts."

"Don't talk," I said, holding her hand. "Dr. Parnell is fantastic. He'll do everything to help your doctor. Between them, they'll save your baby."

"Call Phil," she said when she could talk. She handed me her phone.

I clicked on her husband's number. He answered immediately. I explained what was happening, and he said, "I'll be right there. Let me speak to Danielle."

I handed the phone to her and whatever he said, made her smile in spite of the pain. "Thank you, love," she said and hung up. "He's coming to the . . . ohhhh." She held onto her stomach and moaned.

Please, God, I prayed, *save this baby for Danielle.* He's helped me so many times in my life that I hoped He would come through this time too.

Danielle quieted down for the last few minutes it took to get to the hospital. Mike and Danielle's doctor were waiting at the emergency room entrance. They led the medics carrying Danielle into the hospital.

"Is it okay if I come in, Mike?" I asked him.

"Of course," he said, not looking at me, just clearing the way for Danielle to get into the emergency room.

I sat down on a chair outside the room they put her in and prayed again. Mike wouldn't let anything happen to that baby. If anyone could keep that baby alive, he could. I realized as I sat there that I not only loved this man, I respected his talent as a doctor. He was a life-giving man. A life-saving man. He truly cared for the women who were his patients. He rejoiced with them every time a baby came into this world.

I sat there for an hour, waiting for news.

When Mike came out, he took off his mask. He was smiling.

"The baby decided to stay with his mom," Mike said.

"Oh, Mike," I said, trying to talk through my tears, "thank you."

"I just cleared the way," he said. "It was her doctor who did the real work. He saved the baby."

"How's Danielle?" I asked, dabbing at my eyes with a tissue.

"She's fine," he said. "She wants to see you."

I stood up to go into the room with her.

"I'll take you out of here when you're finished talking to Danielle," Mike said. "Take your time."

I went into the room, and a man with dark hair and kind brown eyes, stood up and held out his hand.

"Are you Mary Louise?" he asked.

I nodded.

"I'm Phil," he said. I shook his hand.

"I'm so glad to meet you," I said. "I've heard so many good things about you."

I went over to the bed and took Danielle's hand.

"Are you okay, Danielle?" I asked.

"Now I am," she said. "I'll never be able to thank you enough for calling Dr. Parnell. My doctor is wonderful, but Dr. Parnell speeded up the whole process. I still have my baby! Thank you, Mary Louise." She pulled my face down to hers and kissed my cheek.

"I'm so glad your baby is all right," I said. "I knew Mike would help."

"Are you in love with him?" Danielle asked.

"Yes," I said. It was the first time I had admitted that to anybody outside of the Hoofers.

"Are you going to marry him?"

Good question. Was I going to divorce George and marry him?

"I'm not sure," I said. "I'm married to someone else."

"Not so easy for you," she said.

"No," I said. "I've been married for thirty years, and we have three children."

"Oh honey, that's a real problem." she said.

"I'll work it out," I said. "You'd better get some rest. I'll see you back at the theater."

"Maybe not," she said. "I think I'm going to quit the show. I don't want to take a chance on losing this baby. I came too close today. I think I'll just stay home and look after Phil."

"Fine with me," he said, leaning over to kiss her.

"Sounds like a good idea to me," I said. "But I'll miss you."

"We can still be friends," she said. "Especially after today." She lowered her voice and pulled me closer. "There's something I need to tell you, Mary Louise. Something about Glenna's death. I have to tell somebody, and I'd like it to be you."

"When you get out of the hospital, we'll talk," I said. "Just get better."

I left the room and Mike was there, waiting to take me back to the theater.

RECIPE FOR CROQUE MADAME

Serves 6

7 T. butter
3 T. flour
2 cups warm milk
12 oz. grated Gruyère cheese
½ cup grated Parmesan cheese
Salt and pepper
Sprinkling of nutmeg
12 slices French bread, toasted
6 T. Dijon mustard
12 slices baked ham
6 eggs

1. Heat broiler.
2. To make sauce, heat three tablespoons of butter in a saucepan, add the flour, and stir until creamy. Add milk and whisk until whole mixture is nice and smooth and bring to a boil. Reduce heat and simmer about six minutes or a little more until thickened. Add a half cup of Gruyère and the half cup Parmesan and whisk until it's all mixed in and is smooth. Season with the salt, pepper and nutmeg.
3. Spread mustard on six slices of the bread and put them on a baking sheet.
4. Put two slices of ham on each piece of bread and sprinkle each one with some of the Gruyère.
5. Broil for about ninety seconds until cheese just begins to melt.
6. Put the other six slices of French bread on top of them, pour the sauce over each one, and

sprinkle with whatever Gruyère and Parmesan are left.

7. Broil about three minutes or less until the bread is lovely and brown and the cheese is melted and bubbly.

8. Fry the eggs in the butter and plop them on top of the divine sandwiches when you take them out of the broiler.

If you make this for lunch, you probably won't need much dinner.

Mary Louise's cooking tip: Marry a man who makes a great chili. Encourage him to make it when you want a night off from cooking.

Chapter 7

When In Doubt, Eat Out

When we got in the cab, I put my arms around Mike and hugged him without saying anything. I couldn't talk. I was close to tears.

"It's okay, honey," he said. "Go ahead and cry if you want."

And I did cry. They were tears of joy for Danielle and for that little baby that would now be born. I cried, too, for not being with this man all the time, not just stolen moments in between rehearsals. I cried because I didn't know how to fix anything.

When I could talk, I said, "Mike, thank you

for saving that baby for Danielle. Thank you for putting up with me when I'm such a coward. I don't know why you don't just tell me to get out of your life and leave you alone."

He kissed me. "Mary Louise. My sweet Mary Louise. The moments I have with you are the best moments of my life. I understand how hard this is for you. I'll wait until you either marry me or tell me you can't see me any more because you're going to stay married to George. In the meantime, I'm just going to love you."

The cab pulled up to the theater, and Mike said, "Tomorrow I'm taking you to walk a labyrinth down by the East River. It will help you put everything in perspective. Have you ever done that?"

"No, I thought you got lost in them. I don't need to get lost any more than I am already."

"You're thinking of a maze," Mike said. "They're different from labyrinths. People often confuse them. Mazes have paths that don't go anywhere, that take you into blind alleys. Labryinths have a path that leads you to the center. A peaceful center. And this one down by the river was designed by my friend Diana Carulli. It's beautiful.

"It sounds wonderful, Mike," I said. "I'd love to go.

"See you tomorrow," he said and kissed me again.

I felt young and happy. When I got back on stage, my friends gathered around me, and I could tell they were relieved at the expression on my face.

"How's Danielle?" Tina asked.

"Did they save the baby?" Pat asked.

"Are you all right?" Janice asked.

I told them Mike and his colleague saved the baby, that Danielle was fine.

"And she said something interesting," I said and lowered my voice. "She said she wanted to tell me something about Glenna's death."

"No kidding!" Gini said. "So when are you going to see her and find out what she meant?" Gini said.

"I told her I'd talk to her when she got out of the hospital."

"You've got to see her right away!" Gini said, raising her voice.

"Gini, she almost lost her baby," I said. "I want to give her time to recover."

I looked behind me and realized that Shelli was hovering in the background. She wasn't usually on stage. I felt uneasy that I had mentioned what Danielle had said. I wasn't sure if she had heard me or not.

I motioned with my head to Gini that Shelli was behind us and she lowered her voice.

"Did you make a date to meet her and talk to her?" Gini said almost in a whisper.

"Not yet," I said, then seeing that Gini was about to explode, I added, "Take it easy, Gini. I'll ask her as soon as she gets out of the hospital and is feeling better."

"Leave her alone, Gini," Tina said, pulling her away from me. She glanced up at Shelli, who had moved closer to us. "Can we do anything for you, Shelli?"

Shelli looked startled. "No, no, I'm fine," she said. "I'm waiting for Marlowe to come back. I guess I'll wait backstage."

"See you tomorrow, then," Tina said. "I'll go find Nevaeh and see if she wants us to do anything more today."

Just then Nevaeh came on stage and asked me if I was all right.

"I'm fine, Nevaeh," I said. "Do you want to rehearse some more?"

"I think we've had enough for one day," she said. "Why don't you Hoofers go home and come back tomorrow for some more Santa."

"Really looking forward to that." Gini said.

"Thanks, Nevaeh," Tina said. "I'll give Peter a call.

After a brief conversation with Peter, she said, "He's in the middle of something he can't leave. He asked if we would mind taking the train home tonight. I told him we'd be glad to."

We all agreed and took a train from Penn Station. I got home around seven. George wasn't there yet.

I poured myself a glass of Chardonnay, and opened *The New York Times* to the crossword puzzle. It was the Wednesday puzzle, so it didn't take me long to finish it. I had just filled in the last word when George opened the door.

"You're late," I said.

"I was working on that damn case," he said. "When did you get home?"

"Not till seven," I said.

"I'm glad you're here," he said. "What's for dinner?"

"I don't really feel like cooking, George," I said. "Let's go to that little restaurant near the station. It's always practically empty, but they've got great food."

"I want to stay home. I've had a rotten day."

"Me too," I said. "I need to go out."

"What do you know about rotten days," he said. "You're just dancing."

"Not today," I said and went to the closet for my coat. "I'll tell you all about it when we get to the restaurant."

He didn't look happy about it but agreed to go.

Twenty minutes later, we were seated in a quiet corner of the Cafe de Maupassant. We were the only people there. It was lovely. No noise. The owner came over to welcome us and wait on us. He handed us menus that promised real French food and reasonably priced wines. Pictures of Paris lined the walls. Two French restaurants in one day. Can't have too many. The owner brought us our wine right away.

I took a sip of my Sauvignon blanc. George raised his glass to me and said, "Here's to you, Mary Louise. No matter how big a grouch I am sometimes, I hope you know how much you mean to me."

"I do know, George," I said. "I appreciate how difficult this case is you're working on now."

"It's not just that," he said. "Lately, you seem

so far away. It's as if you wished you were some-where else."

I looked at this man I had loved for such a long time. This good man who was the father of my three children. The man who would have died for me.

I couldn't tell him about Mike. Not tonight. I'd keep it for another time. I couldn't hurt him.

"I'm sorry, George," I said. "I don't mean to neglect you."

"It's not neglect," he said. "It's like you don't love me anymore."

"Oh, George," I said, reaching across the table to take his hand, "I've just had so many other things on my mind. This job isn't like any of the other gigs we've had. We usually go some-place, dance our feet off, and have a great time. Well, except for the murders."

"What's different about this one?" he asked.

"Well, take today as an example," I said. "We were ready to exercise to strengthen our mus-cles when the Rockette who was telling us what to do—her name is Danielle—suddenly dou-bled over in pain. It turned out she was preg-nant, and it looked like she was about to lose her baby. We called the ambulance, and I went to the emergency room with her."

"For God's sake, Mary Louise," he said. "What happened?"

I told him the whole story, and he was about to explode into a rant about my life as a dancer when the owner came back to take our order. We were still the only people in the restaurant.

"Is it always this quiet?" I asked him.

"It gets more crowded later on," he said. "It's still pretty early."

I thought seven-thirty was when most people had dinner, but I didn't want to say anything. It was obvious that not as many people liked French food as much as we did.

I ordered a veal cordon bleu. It's sort of a veal sandwich and one of my favorite dishes. I knew it was very good at this restaurant. George ordered a *blanquette de veau* and managed to calm down enough to talk to me rationally.

"I don't see why you thought you had to go to the hospital with her. You barely know her. Couldn't one of her friends have gone with her?"

"Well . . ." I didn't want to go into the whole thing about Mike and how I called him and how he made everything go faster.

"There's something else, George," I said. "She said she had something to tell me about Glenna's death, that she had to tell somebody. She chose me."

"Please, Mary Louise," he said. "Stay out of this. You don't really know what happened to Glenna."

"I won't take any unnecessary chances, George. Don't worry. She probably doesn't really know anything significant about Glenna's death. But I do want to find out what she meant. Gini said she started to say something about it the other day but was too afraid to talk."

"Let Gini go talk to her then."

"Danielle said she wanted to talk to me, not Gini."

"What exactly did Gini say she started to say?" George asked.

"Gini said she kept repeating, 'I didn't *do* anything."

"That doesn't mean she knows who did it," George said with an impatient wave of his hand. "You women are just making up something out of nothing."

"That's what Peter said," I said and took a bite of my cordon bleu the waiter had just put down in front of me. It was sublime. A little veal sandwich filled with some kind of divine melted cheese and ham.

"How come you were the one who went to the hospital with Danielle, anyway," George asked again, taking a mouthful of his *blanquette* and pouring me a glass of wine. "Why didn't one of the other Rockettes go with her?"

"Danielle was rehearsing us," I said. "There weren't any other Rockettes around. I couldn't let her go alone. It's too frightening going to the emergency room by yourself."

"So you went to the hospital with her and waited all by yourself while they treated her? None of your friends were with you, either?"

I took a sip of my wine. "Just me," I said. I'm not very good at lying. I hated not telling George the truth. I would have to tell him about Mike soon, but I couldn't do it on this evening sitting across the table from him in this lovely restaurant. I asked George about his case to change the subject and managed to stay off the subject of Danielle and the hospital for the rest of our meal.

Our dinner was delicious and the tables gradually filled up with other customers. Our whole meal was a blessed respite from what had happened in New York that day.

I fell asleep in George's arms that night.

RECIPE FOR VEAL CORDON BLEU

Serves 4

8 thin slices of veal cutlet
8 slices Gruyere cheese
4 thin slices baked ham
1 cup Panko
2 tsp. salt
¾ tsp. ground black pepper
¾ cup flour
2 large eggs
2 T. butter
2 T. olive oil

1. Make four sandwiches of veal cutlets filling each one with a slice of ham and two slices of cheese.
2. Line up three dishes. Put flour, salt, and pepper in the first dish; eggs, salt and pepper in the second dish; and panko, salt, and pepper in the third.
3. Dip the sandwiches in the flour, then the eggs, then the panko. Put them in the fridge until you're ready to cook them.
4. Cook the veal sandwiches in the butter and olive oil until they're brown and the cheese melts, turning them once, about five minutes altogether.

Expect all kinds of oohs and aahs when you serve this.

RECIPE FOR BLANQUETTE DE VEAU

Serves 6

2 lb. veal cut up into cubes
14 whole little white onions, peeled
Parsley
1 stalk celery
1 leek
1 bay leaf
1 clove garlic
¼ tsp. peppercorns
¼ tsp. thyme
2 tsp. salt
2 T. butter, softened
2 T. flour
1 cup heavy cream
2 egg yolks
¾ cup mushrooms sautéed in butter

1. Boil the veal briefly in water in a deep pot for five minutes. Drain.
2. Fill the pot with the meat in it with four cups of water, the carrots, and the little white onions.
3. Make a bouquet garni, filling a cheesecloth bag with the parsley, celery, leek, bay leaf, garlic, peppercorns, and thyme, and put the tied-up bag in the pot with the meat. Add the salt and simmer the whole thing until the veal is tender, about two hours. *Take out the veal, carrots, and onions, but do not throw away the water.*
4. Keep the veal, carrots, and onions warm. Throw out the bouquet garni.
5. Boil the water that you simmered the veal in,

and carefully saved, until it's reduced about two-thirds.

6. Cream the butter with the flour and add it to the water. Boil for about a minute, stirring constantly all the while.

7. Mix the eggs yolks and cream together and add it to the thickened broth, again stirring constantly until you have a nice thick cream sauce. *Do not boil, though, or it will curdle. Just cook gently.*

8. You now have one of the best-tasting sauces ever made to pour over your veal, carrots, and onions you kept warm.

9. Toss on the buttery mushrooms and you have a meal fit for your best friends.

10. Serve with rice or mashed potatoes and a lovely salad.

(May I come to dinner? I love this dish!)

Mary Louise's cooking tip: When in doubt, go to a website such as Allrecipes.com to find the perfect way to cook that meat or fish.

Chapter 8

Get Me My Lawyer

The next day, Peter was there bright and early, and I ran out to join my friends who were, as usual, full of questions.

"So are you going to find out what Danielle meant about Glenna's murder today?" Gini asked.

I hesitated, George's warnings bouncing around in my head. "Well, maybe not today, but . . ."

"What day then?" Gini yelped. "Next Christmas?"

"Calm down, Gini," Tina said. "I'm sure Mary

Louise will talk to her when she feels she's recovered from almost losing her baby. Maybe at the next rehearsal."

"She said she wasn't coming back to the theater," I said. "She's afraid the same thing will happen again if she exercises too strenuously, and she'll lose the baby. I think her days as a Rockette are over."

"Well, if she isn't coming back to the theater, when do you expect to see her?" Gini asked.

"Oh, I don't know," I said, moving farther away from my persistent questioner. "I'll figure something out. We have no idea what really happened to Glenna. Danielle said she wanted to talk to me about her death, not her murder. Anyway, if you're so anxious to find out what she has to say, why don't you ask her? Call her up."

"She obviously wants to tell you," Gini said. "You got Mike to help her, and she's grateful."

"I know," I said. "Could we talk about something else—please, Gini!"

Tina gestured to Gini to back off, and Gini sputtered into silence.

"You'll figure it out, Weezie," Tina said. "Take your time."

I smiled at her. I'm always grateful to Tina for her thoughtfulness.

"Hold it, ladies," Peter said, almost bumping into the curb as he backed out of the driveway. "What's all this about Danielle and Glenna's death?" He looked accusingly at Tina in the front seat next to him. "You never tell me anything," he said.

"Oh, Peter, I forgot," she said. "Danielle said she wanted to tell Mary Louise something about Glenna's death, but we have no idea what it is."

"Careful, Weezie," he said. "I wouldn't get involved in this if I were you."

"That's what George said," I told him. "I won't take any chances, Peter. Don't worry."

Tina leaned over the front seat to talk to me. "What if she tells you one of the Rockettes did it? If you find out who did it, they might try to kill you."

"If she tells me that, I'll go straight to the police," I said. "I'm not going to hang around to get killed."

"She probably won't tell you who did it," Pat said. "I got the impression the other day that she just wants to make sure we know she didn't have anything to do with it."

"Do be careful, though, Weezie," Gini said. "We'd hate to lose you. It's hard to get a substitute Santa at the last minute."

I punched her lightly, causing her to spill a little of her coffee.

"No really, Weez," she said. "Don't take any chances, okay?

"I'll be all right, you old worrywart," I said and put a couple of sugars in my own coffee. "Now let's talk about something else. Something good."

"Want to hear about where Tom and I are going to get married?" Janice asked.

"Oh yes, Jan," I said, so glad to have a change of subject. "Where? Tell us."

"Have you ever seen that old boat moored in Brooklyn—near that really good restaurant, The River Cafe? Near the carousel. You know."

"You mean Bargemusic," Tina said. "It's a wonderful boat. Is that where you're getting married?"

"Yes," Janice said, her face reflecting her delight. "It's perfect for our wedding. We went over to see it yesterday and talked to the owner, who is really nice."

"When are you doing this?" Pat asked.

"Probably next spring some time," Janice said. "We're going to go on our honeymoon first."

That was so Janice.

"Why?" Pat asked.

"No special reason," Janice said. "We just want to have time together, and we figured we don't have to be married to do that."

"Where are you going?" I asked. I would never go on my honeymoon before the wedding, but I loved the fact that Janice would.

"We thought we'd go to London and see as many plays as we can find. They're doing *Death of a Salesman* there now and, believe it or not, *Jersey Boys*. They really love American plays. It costs less to see most of them there than here."

"Sounds great, Jan," Gini said. "Mind if I come along?"

Jan laughed. "I do mind. Much as I love you, Gini, I think I'll just go on my honeymoon with Tom. You'll be in India getting your little girl anyway, won't you?"

"I hope so," Gini said, holding up her hand with her fingers crossed. "It looks that way. Alex and his friend at the *Times* have been working on it, and I think we're going over there after our dance with the Rockettes is done."

"Knowing Alex," Peter said, "he'll never stop until you have your little girl."

"Oh thank you for that, Peter," Gini said, kissing him on the ear. "I'm so afraid to hope."

We were all quiet, thinking our own private thoughts. I realized I dreaded this day coming up. I usually love our dancing jobs, but this one wasn't fun. I wondered if I was the only one who felt like that. I didn't want to sound like a spoiled brat. I hesitated. I hate saying negative things. It's just the way I am. But I had to say something.

"Could I ask . . ." I said, "I mean . . . you know how much I love to dance. But is anyone else having as tough a time as I am rehearsing that darn Santa Claus thing? I know they're perfectionists, those Rockettes, and we're lucky to be dancing with them, and all that, but I'm not having any fun at all. It's hard work, and I'll be glad when we're finished. I've never felt that way before in any of our other jobs."

"I know what you mean, Weez," Tina said. "It's definitely harder than any other kind of dancing we've done, but we knew that going in—how perfect they were, I mean. You don't want to quit, do you?"

"I guess not," I said. "If everybody else wants to keep on with this, I will too."

"To tell you the truth, I don't like it either," Janice said. "But I love being able to tell people that we're dancing with the Rockettes. Everyone's always impressed. Me too."

"What about you, Gini?" I asked the most honest person I know.

"It stinks," she said. "I'm not having any fun either, Weezie, but it's too late to back out now. We took the job and we've got to stay till the end. Besides I want to find out who killed Glenna—don't you?"

"I'd just as soon read about it in the papers after they catch the killer," I said.

"It's only a couple of months, Mary Louise," Pat said. "And I love coming into New York every day. There's so much to do there. I get to see Denise, and now David, much more than I would otherwise because he has a week off from school."

"What are you and Denise and David going to do today?" I asked. I loved seeing Pat's face light up whenever she talked about those two. They were obviously as precious to her as she was to them.

"Well, I know this sounds hokey," she said, "but David and I are leaving Denise behind and going on a Circle Line cruise around Manhattan. He's never done it before and, believe it or not, neither have I. I always thought it was too touristy a thing to do, but now I'll see it through David's eyes, and it won't be touristy at all."

"I wish I could go with you," I said.

"Come with us," she said. "We'd love to have you."

I wasn't sure, but I thought I might be having that conversation with Danielle today, so I said, "Maybe next time, Pat."

Tina said she was going to consult Andrea

again about reception plans at the Frick. Then she grabbed my hand.

"Really, Mary Louise," she said, "Go right to the police if Danielle tells you anything crucial. Don't go back to the theater."

"I'll be fine," I said, smiling at her.

We arrived at the theater and Peter put his hand on my arm as I was getting out of the car. "You have my number on your cell, right?" he said. "Call me if you need me. Anytime. I mean it."

I kissed the top of his head. "Thanks, Peter," I said. "I do have your number, but I'll be all right." I didn't really think I was in any danger. I always try to think positively.

We went into the theater. By now the teenaged ticket taker barely gave us a glance. Marlowe, Nevaeh, Andrea, and Shelli were all on stage waiting for us.

"How's Danielle?" Marlowe asked.

"Doing well," I said, wary. I never quite trusted Marlowe.

"She's not here today," Marlowe said. "How long are they going to keep her in the hospital?"

"They'll probably let her out today," I said. "But she said she didn't think she would dance anymore. She was afraid she might lose her baby."

"It would be nice if she shared that information with me," Marlowe said. "I was counting on her to rehearse you hoofers. I'll have to get someone else."

She pointed to the Santa Claus jackets.

"Get into your costumes." She stopped, looked at Shelli and then said to me, "Is it true that Danielle said something to you about Glenna's death?"

I was halfway into my Santa jacket, so I mumbled, "Oh, probably nothing important," with my head under the fat suit.

"I would think anything to do with Glenna's unfortunate death would be very important," Marlowe said when I pulled the suit on.

"I don't know how important it is," I said. "I won't be able to see her for a while, anyway, with our rehearsals and her being at home and all."

"I'd appreciate it if you'd tell me anything she has to tell you," Marlowe said.

Oh sure! I thought. *I'll rush right back here the minute she tells me who killed Glenna.*

"Yes, of course," I said. I realized Shelli must have overheard me telling my friends what Danielle said and told Marlowe. "She probably just wants to thank me for going to the emergency room with her. My friend is the head obstetrician at New York Hospital, and he probably got help for her faster than her own doctor could have."

"Mmm-hmm," Marlowe said. She turned her attention to the rest and made sure they all had their Santa jackets on. "Nevaeh will put you through your paces today," she said. "How are you doing with the Santa suits?"

"Terribly!" Gini said. "They're the worst things I've ever danced in."

"Get used to them," Marlowe said. "You're going to spend a lot of time in them."

"Terrific," Gini said.

"There is one good thing about them," Nevaeh said, trying to lighten the mood.

"What's that?" Gini said.

"I lose ten pounds every season after dancing in those things," she said. We believed her. She was slim as a bathing-suit model.

"Better get started," Marlowe said, and left the stage, followed by Shelli.

My phone vibrated just before we started to dance. It was Danielle.

"I'm back home, Mary Louise," she said "Can you come for lunch today? I really need to talk to you." Her tone was urgent.

"Yes, of course I'll come. How's twelve-thirty? We should be through being tortured by then. Are you sure you feel up to this?"

"I'm fine," she said. "Phil has been taking good care of me. You and I will be alone at lunch. Do me a favor and don't mention that you're coming here."

"Tell me your address, Danielle."

She gave me an address on Fifteenth Street between Fifth and Sixth. I promised to be there as soon as the morning's rehearsal was over.

"What was that all about?" Gini asked.

I pulled her away from Nevaeh. "I'm going to Danielle's for lunch. She said she needed to talk to me."

"Good!" Gini said. "You'll find out who killed Glenna."

"Nobody said Glenna was killed, Gini! She just said she wanted to talk to me. That's all."

"Want me to come with you?"

"Thanks, but she said not to tell anyone else I was coming."

"Let me know if you change your mind."

"Thanks, Gini," I said. "I wish I could take you along. Everyone keeps telling me not to get involved."

"I just hope you know what you're doing," Gini said. "I'm the one who keeps pushing you to find out what she has to say. I'll never forgive myself if anything happens to you."

"Nothing's going to happen to me, Gini," I said. "Don't worry."

"Of course I'll worry," she said. "That's what I do best. But be careful, hon, okay?"

"Count on it," I said and picked up my phone to call Mike.

I told him what had happened. "Can we do the labyrinth tomorrow?" I asked. "I really want to do that."

"Of course," he said. "Call me when you get back and tell me what she said."

The Santa suits seemed a little more manageable on this day, and the rehearsal went fairly quickly. Some leg-raises, bicycle pumping, treadmilling and push-ups, and Nevaeh told us to come back at two.

I left the theater and took a taxi to Fifteenth Street.

When I got to Danielle's building, the street outside was full of police cars. The door was blocked by a police officer who told me I couldn't go in the building.

"Why, what's wrong?" I asked. "I'm supposed

to have lunch with a friend of mine in this building."

"What's her name?" he asked, pulling out his iPhone.

"Danielle Jennings," I said.

He was instantly more alert, tense. "What is your relationship to Ms. Jennings?" he asked.

"She's a friend," I said, beginning to realize something was very wrong. "Why? Did she have to go back to the hospital?"

"When was she in the hospital?" he asked.

This was all too weird. "She was in the hospital yesterday because she almost lost . . . Why are you asking me all these questions? What's going on here?"

"There has been an accident. Ms. Jennings fell or jumped or was pushed out of her window."

"My God," I said, "is she still alive?"

"I can't give you any more information," the officer said. "I need your name and the reason you were coming to see her."

"I'm Mary Louise Temple. I told you—I'm here to have lunch with her. I wanted to be sure she was all right."

"Why wouldn't she be all right?"

"Because of the baby. Because she almost lost . . ." I stopped. I had learned one thing from being married to a lawyer all these years: Don't say any more than you have to when someone starts questioning you.

"May I go, officer?" I asked. "I have to get back to rehearsal."

"You're a Rockette too?" he asked. "Like Mrs. Jennings?"

"No, no," I said. "I'm just a dancer. But we're dancing with the Rockettes in their Christmas show."

"I think you'd better stay here," the officer said. "The detective may want to ask you some more questions."

"All right," I said. "I'll call my husband and ask him to meet me here. He's a lawyer."

"Why do you need a lawyer?" he said.

"It's not that I *need* a lawyer," I said, "but I'll feel better if he's here."

He led me to a place near the entrance to Danielle's building and told me to make my call and to stay there. When I was through, he would take me upstairs to her apartment where the detective was in charge. He was nice enough, but I couldn't shake the feeling that I was under arrest for something. I knew I couldn't just walk away.

I called George and told him what had happened.

"I told you this would happen, Mary Louise," he said. "Didn't I tell you not to get mixed up in all this?"

"Yes, you did, George," I said. "But I need you to get over here now to make sure I don't say anything I shouldn't."

"Luckily, I'm in New York today," he said. "I'll be right there."

I hung up and clicked on Tina's number.

"Hey, Weez," she said, "How's your lunch with Danielle? Did you find out anything?"

"Oh Tina," I said, and then couldn't talk.

"What is it, Mary Louise? What's the matter?"

"It's Danielle," I said and choked on the words. "She either fell or was pushed out the window of her apartment. I don't even know if she's still alive."

"What!" Tina cried. "What happened?"

I told her what the officer had told me. "That's all I know. I just hope they don't arrest me because I was coming here to see her."

"Are they keeping you there?" she asked. "Want me to call Peter?"

"No, that's okay," I said. "George is in New York today, and I'm waiting for him to come and get me out of here."

"Thank goodness," she said. "I'm glad George is going to be with you. Call me back as soon as you can."

When I hung up, the police officer took my arm again. "Detective Carver wants to talk to you," he said. "Come with me to Ms. Jennings' apartment."

"How will my husband know where to find me?" I asked.

"I'll be here when he comes. I'll bring him to you."

The lobby of her building was large and bare, with a desk in the middle where a man checked visitors in. He was talking to another policeman, and we walked by him to the bank of elevators in the back.

We went up to the twelfth floor, where two policemen were stationed outside her apartment. They opened the door for us, and I walked into Danielle's living room. Detective Carver was waiting for me.

"Ms. Rogers," he said, "we meet again. I understand you were planning to have lunch with Ms. Jennings today. Would you mind answering a few questions?"

"I don't have any choice, do I, Detective?" I said.

"Afraid not," he said.

"Could you please wait until my husband gets here?" I said. "He's a lawyer, and I'd feel better if he were here with me."

"If you think you need a lawyer," he said, "I'll wait."

This was not going well. I sounded guilty, even to myself. But guilty of what?

"As I told the policeman downstairs," I said, "it's not that I *need* a lawyer, I just want my husband here with me."

"I understand," the Detective said and told me to have a seat.

I sat down on the white couch across from the floor-to-ceiling windows. I was overwhelmed by the view. The apartment faced the Empire State building a few blocks to the northeast. There it was, one of the most famous buildings in the world that many visitors to New York came to see, rising regally above the other buildings in the city, showing off its spire against the sky.

"What a great apartment," I said to the detective.

"Yes it is," he said. "They must have paid a lot to get a view like that."

"I suppose so. Both of them earned good salaries, I guess." I realized Phil was not there. "Where is her husband?"

"He went with the medics who took her body to the hospital."

"Her body?" I said. "Then she's dead." It was the first time anyone actually confirmed it.

"Yes, she was pushed out the window."

"Poor Phil," I said. "He loved her so much. And she was going to have a . . ." I couldn't finish.

"He was really broken up," Carver said. "I felt really sorry for him."

The door of the apartment opened. The policeman who had brought me up here reappeared with George, who hurried into the room.

"Are you all right?" he asked me.

"I am now," I said. "I'm so glad to see you."

George turned to Detective Carver. "Why have you brought my wife up here?"

"She came to have lunch with Ms. Jennings. I thought perhaps she could shed some light on her death. We're not accusing her of anything, Mr. . . . ?"

"Temple. George Temple. My wife barely knew Ms. Jennings. She helped her the other day at the hospital when she almost lost her baby. I guess Ms. Jennings wanted to thank her. That's all."

"I'm sure you understand, Mr. Temple, that we are trying to get as much information as we can about Danielle Jennings' death. We hoped your wife could help."

"I'd be glad to tell you anything that would

help," I said. "I just don't know very much about her."

"Why did she ask you to come to lunch? Was it just to thank you or was there some other reason?"

I hesitated, looked at George who shook his head. I got it. Don't say anything, Mary Louise. "She didn't really say anything, Detective," I said. "It was the tone of her voice. She said she had to tell me something, and she sounded urgent. Oh, and she told me not to tell anybody I was coming here."

"And did you?" the detective asked.

"Only one of my friends," I said. "She wanted to come with me, and I had to tell her I wasn't supposed to tell anyone I was coming here."

"Which friend?"

"Excuse me, officer," George said. "I don't see how that is relevant to Ms. Jennings death. My wife has told you all she knows."

"She is free to leave, Mr. Temple. I have no more questions."

I stood up. Good old George. "I'm sorry about Danielle, Detective," I said. "She was a nice woman. I hope you find out what happened to her."

"Thank you, Ms. Temple. I will have some questions for you later."

"Of course," I said.

George led me out of the apartment, and we took the elevator down to the lobby and out to the street.

"Do you want to get some lunch before you go back to the theater?" he asked me.

I took his arm. "Thank you George. I'm not at all hungry. But I don't have to be back at the theater for another hour. Want to walk down to Washington Square?"

"Sure," he said. "Come on."

We walked over to Fifth Avenue and headed down toward the arch that towers over the square and marks the beginning of Fifth Avenue.

"I'm so glad you're here, George. Thank you for coming so fast. How come you're in New York today?"

"One of the witnesses in the Alderson case works in the city and I came over to interview her."

"Was she a help?"

"Actually, she was. She lives in the building where the accident happened. Once when she rang for the elevator, the doors opened and there was no car, just an empty hole. She was lucky she didn't fall in the way Alderson did. She notified the owner of the building who said he would have the elevator people fix it. Obviously they didn't."

"Sounds like she'll really be able to help you."

"I hope so," he said. "I'm glad I was in the city today."

"Me too!" I said, squeezing his arm.

We walked along past the elegant apartment houses and hotels lining lower Fifth Avenue. This is one of my favorite places in New York City. After James, my oldest child, was born, I used to walk down here, wheeling him in his carriage. I would sit on the edge of the fountain behind the arch and listen to the guitar players and talk to the other mothers enjoying the life bustling around us in this park, which was full of college students and harmless idlers lazing away their days. I munched on a hot dog I bought at one of the carts and James sucked on his bottle of milk until he fell asleep. Both of us were totally content.

"Remember when I used to come here with James?" I asked George.

"Those were good days," George said. "Do you ever wish we'd stayed in the city?"

"Not really," I said. "The children were better off growing up in Champlain. I'm glad I had those first few years here though. I love this city. It was so much fun eating in different restaurants and going to plays and museums. There was always something new and interesting going on."

"Maybe I could meet you after your rehearsals on the days I'm in New York and we could do all that again," George said.

"Think we've still got the energy for that after I've been dancing all day and you've been looking down elevator shafts?" I asked.

"You're still the youngest person I know," he said. "I always feel younger when I'm with you."

I let go of his arm and did a quick tap dance step on the sidewalk. A young guy with a beard and torn jeans walking by said, "You go, girl." He made me laugh.

"She's mine," George said and pulled me into the park behind the arch.

On this day, it was still full of students and mothers with carriages. I was startled to see a man seated at a grand piano in the middle of the sidewalk. He was playing with full force and skill, right there in the park. People dropped money in a box on the piano but nothing distracted him from his fierce and powerful performance.

We sat down on a bench to listen.

"I wonder who he is," I said.

"I read about him in the *Times*," George said. "He plays here a few times a week. He once worked for a ballet company, I think. But he got tired of it and started playing the piano all over the city until he finally settled on Washington Park as his regular place. The donations people give him pay his expenses and he's happy with that."

I leaned back against George's arm and closed my eyes. The music soared over and around and through me.

"What is that he's playing?" I asked. "I've heard it so many times but I can't think of what it's called."

"It's Rachmaninoff's Piano Concerto no. 3," he said. George listens to classical music all the time and always knows stuff like that. His wide range of interests was one of the things that made me fall in love him in the first place. There were lots of other things about George that I treasured: his sense of humor, his brilliance, his fierce desire to use his legal training to help other people, his desire to travel and see as much of the world as he could, his appreciation of good food, his love of life.

I wanted to share all those things with him when we were married. I encouraged him to use his law degree to do the most good he could in this life. We were a team in those days. He defended people who couldn't afford attorneys. I worked to set up programs for women in prison. Lately, he seemed to have lost all of his fierce love of life. Today a little of it was back again.

We sat there until the pianist finished. When he stopped, George pulled me close to him and said, "I'm so glad I have you, Mary Louise. I can't imagine life without you. I know I forget to tell you that sometimes, but I hope you know what you mean to me."

"Thank you for being here today, George," I said. "You're always there when I need you." It hit me how true that was. He'd never let me down when I needed him all through the years.

I hugged him and stood up. "I'd better get back to the theater. We're supposed to be back by two."

He got up and dropped some money in the box on the piano as we walked past it. He took me over to a cab parked nearby. "Be careful," he said.

Mary Louise's cooking tip: If you think somebody is trying to kill you, go to the police station for dinner.

Chapter 9

Follow The Pretty Blue Path

When I got back to the theater my friends were all waiting to hear what had happened. Tina had told them Danielle was dead, but they didn't know any of the details.

I told them that the detective said she was pushed out the window.

"She knew who killed Glenna," Gini said. "Somebody wanted her dead before she told someone." She looked at me. "Like you, for instance, Weez. They didn't want her telling you who did it over lunch."

I shivered. "Good thing she never got to tell

me," I said. "I might have followed her out that window."

"You still might," Gini said. "Whoever killed her probably thinks you know more than you do."

"Gee, thanks, Gini," I said. "What a comforting thought."

"Gini, do you ever stop and think before you say something like that?" Tina said.

"Well, I'm just telling Weezie the truth," Gini said. "You do want to know the truth, don't you, Buttercup?"

"Not when it involves my possible murder," I said. "I'd just as soon not think about that."

Nevaeh ran over to our group huddled on the side of the stage.

"Is it true, Mary Louise?" she asked. "Did somebody kill Danielle?"

"It looks that way," I said. "Detective Carver told me she had been pushed out the window."

"Do they have any suspects?" Nevaeh asked. She kept twisting her scarf as she talked to us.

"They are investigating," I said. "I thought they were going to arrest me when I showed up for lunch. Luckily, George was in town and came to get me."

"George comes in handy, doesn't he?" Pat asked.

I knew what she meant and just nodded. I knew that wasn't all George meant to me. He wasn't just a safety net, someone to take care of me. Not as long as he can identify Rachmaninoff's Piano Concerto No. 3 played in the middle of Washington Square Park. Not as long as he made me feel like I was the only woman in the world who mattered to him.

Marlowe came on stage.

"How was your lunch with Danielle, Ms. Temple?" she asked.

Ms. Temple?

"Didn't anyone tell you, Marlowe?" I said. "Danielle is dead."

"What do you mean she's dead?" Marlowe said. "I just talked to her on the phone this morning. How could she be dead?"

"She was found dead on the sidewalk under her window, twelve stories down." I said.

"She must have jumped," Marlowe said. "She was afraid she'd lose her baby and killed herself. How terrible."

"The police think she was pushed," I said.

"I'll call her husband and tell him how sorry I am," Marlowe said and left the stage.

I knew there was no way Marlowe wouldn't have known about Danielle's death. The first place the police would have called would be the Music Hall.

"Let's work on that Santa routine some more," Nevaeh said, "Try to . . . she stopped, put her hands over her face. "It's no use. I can't do this today. I'm too upset about Danielle. She was a good friend."

"It's okay, Nevaeh," Tina said. "We worked on it this morning. Why don't we take a break and do this tomorrow. Maybe Andrea could take over for you."

"She's usually at the Frick," Nevaeh said. "She

spends as little time here as possible. I don't blame her. Rehearsing was fun when Glenna was in charge. Now it's sort of grim. Two of us dead. You're right, Tina. Why don't you guys take the rest of the day off? I'll be all right tomorrow."

"I'm so sorry, Nevaeh," Tina said. "I know she was a good friend of yours. Tomorrow will be fine."

Tina told us to meet her in front of the theater at five, as usual, for the ride home. She and the others all scattered to take advantage of a free afternoon in New York. I folded up my Santa outfit and gathered my things. There was still time to walk that labyrinth with Mike. I was really curious about it.

I clicked on his number. He answered right away.

"What's up, babe?"

"Seems I'm free to walk that labyrinth with you if you still want to," I said.

"Of course I want to," he said. "What happened to your lunch with Danielle?"

"She's dead."

"What do you mean, she's dead?" Mike asked. "What happened to her?"

"Somebody pushed her out her window— that's what we think happened—and she was killed."

"I'm coming to get you," he said. "Stay right there."

I hung up the phone and was putting on comfortable shoes when Nevaeh came over and sat down very close to me.

"I know how much you helped Danielle, Mary

Louise," she said in a very low voice. "I went to the hospital to see her, and she told me what you did for her."

"I was glad I could help," I said. "I didn't really do anything, though. It was my friend Dr. Parnell and her doctor who saved her baby."

"I know," Nevaeh said, "but you were the one who called him and stayed there in the hospital until you knew she was all right."

She looked as if she wanted to say more but wasn't sure if she should.

"Was there something else you wanted to tell me?" I asked.

"Well," she said, in an even softer voice, "did she tell you anything about Glenna's death when you saw her in the hospital?"

Uh-oh. Am I going to find out more than I wanted to know about Glenna's death? Again?

"No," I said. "She didn't tell me anything in the hospital." I started to get up to leave the stage and this uncomfortable conversation, but Nevaeh put her hand on my arm.

"Don't go, Mary Louise," she said. "I want to tell you something about Glenna and what happened to her. I've carried it around with me long enough. I've got to tell somebody."

I knew I should jump up and run out of there like all my friends had told me to do, but I really wanted to hear what Nevaeh had to say. There seemed to be quite a few people who knew something about this murder, and I did want to find out more. In spite of all the warnings from people I loved, my curiosity was stronger than all their words of caution. I have this love of solving mysteries. I always take along a stack of murder mysteries to read when we go to Cape Cod for our vacation.

"Do you know who killed Glenna?" I asked.

She looked around, then whispered, "It wasn't just one person. There were . . ."

"Meow."

Ranger appeared out of nowhere. She jumped up on Nevaeh's lap and bumped her furry face against Nevaeh's.

"Ranger!" she said. "Where did you come from?"

Ranger meowed a couple more times, and then a familiar voice said, "What happened to the rehearsal, Nevaeh?"

Marlowe was standing in back of us. Neither of us had heard her come on stage, but Ranger must have seen her and jumped up on Nevaeh's lap. She was trying to warn us. What a smart little cat. I reached over to pat her and she purred.

"Oh, hello Marlowe," Nevaeh said. "I didn't hear you come in. We decided—because of Danielle—that we'd postpone the rehearsal until tomorrow. It was just too hard."

"Yes, yes, tragic," Marlowe said, her voice totally unemotional. "But, as they say, the show must go on. What were you and Little Miss Muffet talking about?"

"Oh, um, nothing really. Just stuff about the rehearsal tomorrow morning and how to dance with those heavy jackets. Like that."

"Well, I think we should let our little Hoofer get on with her life," Marlowe said. "See you tomorrow, Ms. Temple."

I stood up, glad to be getting out of here.

"And get rid of that cat," Marlowe said to Nevaeh.

Ranger slid down off of Nevaeh's lap and scurried offstage.

I ran up the aisle and glanced back before I went out into the lobby. Marlowe was talking to Nevaeh, who was listening, head bowed, her body bent over. I felt like I should stay and help Nevaeh, but I wasn't sure what I could do. I left.

A cab pulled up to the curb and Mike called to me from the back seat.

"Over here, Mary Louise," he said.

I jumped in the cab with him, and he said, "Now tell me exactly what happened with Danielle."

The cab headed east toward the FDR Drive, and I told Mike the whole weird story about arriving for lunch and being questioned by the police and George coming to rescue me and—

"George was there?" he said. "I thought George worked in New Jersey."

I explained about the woman and the elevator shaft. I skipped over the part where George and I went to Washington Square and listened to a piano player in the middle of the park.

"Lawyers come in handy," he said.

I didn't say anything.

Mike told the driver to get off the drive at the end of Houston Street. We walked across a ramp and Mike took my hand to lead me down a path to an amazing sight on the ground next to the East River.

"Oh Mike, it's beautiful!" I said

There, surrounded by acacia trees, was a huge blue, red, and yellow labyrinth. I let go of his hand and ran over to look more closely at this unbelievable pocket of quiet and wonder in the busiest city in the world.

The path winding around and around the labyrinth was painted blue, outlined in yellow. It looked like ocean waves lapping gently at the people who walked on it. In the very middle was a red and silver center. An orange circle surrounded the labyrinth and painted in big letters on the circle was the reason I was there: "Come. Let us be in beauty together circled by trees as the river flows."

"Those are Diana's words," Mike said. "Diana Carulli. You know, I told you she designed this labyrinth. There are labyrinths designed by Diana all over the world. You have to meet her. She's a remarkable woman."

I looked at Mike. I couldn't believe this miracle. "Can I . . ."

"Go ahead," he said. "I'll be right here."

I took my first step onto the blue path of the labyrinth and followed it around and around, looking down, lost in my own thoughts as I wound my way to the center. I felt like I was wading through the ocean near the shore where it was calm and soothing. Every once in a while a boat whistle sounded, a background to my reverie.

All other sounds of the city were hushed as I concentrated on that path and on what mattered most to me. My husband and my children. The more I walked and looked down, shutting out the buildings, the trees, the boats, the cars, other people, the closer I got to my true feelings about those four people I loved. I adored my children. They had brought me the most precious moments of my life as they grew and learned to take care of themselves.

I did what I could to help them over the rough spots, but I knew they had to learn to figure them out without my help. I wouldn't be with them forever. As I walked along this path, I knew they would be all right. But George? I couldn't get a clear feeling about George. I certainly loved him when we were in Washington Square. What if I did leave him for Mike? Would I be happier?

When I finally reached the red and silver center of the labyrinth, I still had no answer to this question, but something had happened to my soul. When I looked up and saw the river nearby, the sky above me, I knew that whatever I decided, I would know how to handle it. It was the first time I knew that for sure. I realized that I had been through enough turns and twists in this life of mine that I would be all right. What an amazing feeling. Just from walking this labyrinth.

I took a deep breath and followed the ocean path back the way I had come, much lighter of heart than when I went in, until I reached the beginning. Mike was waiting there for me. He could tell from my face that I had come out of that labyrinth a different person than when I went in.

He didn't say anything. He just put his arm around me and gently guided me toward the river.

"How do you feel?" he asked me.

"Peaceful," I said. "It's the first time I've felt this way in a long time. As if everything was going to be all right. I've been so worried."

"About us?" he asked.

"Yes," I said. "I don't know what to do about us, Mike. One minute I'm sure I want to leave George and be with you. The next minute I think I want to work things out with George. I know how hard this is for you and I'm so sorry to keep going back and forth like this."

He held me close and kissed my forehead.

"Did you figure out what to do while you were walking the labyrinth?" he asked. "You said you felt peaceful."

"I didn't actually decide," I said. "But I felt that whatever I decided I would know how to handle it."

"I'm sure you will know," he said. "And don't worry, darling. I'm willing to wait until you make up your mind."

I looked up into those kind brown eyes and smiled at him.

"Thank you for your understanding, Mike," I said. "And thank you for this labyrinth today. I want to walk more of them."

"They're everywhere," he said. "We'll do this again."

I pulled away from him. "I should get back to the theater. Peter's going to pick us up."

He took my face in his hands and said, "Whatever you decide, sweetheart, I will love you no matter what. I know how hard this is for you, and if you decide to stay with George, I will still be your friend for the rest of your life. If you ever need me for any reason, all you need to do is pick up the phone and call me. I'll be there."

"Oh Mike," I said and reached up to kiss him. "I love you."

"I know," he said.

He took my hand and led me back up to the street where he hailed a cab.

As I got into the cab, Mike said, "Remember Auden's words, Mary Louise: 'Dance till the stars come down with the rafters.' "

"Dance, dance, dance until you drop," I said, finishing the quote.

When I got back to the theater, I expected to see my friends waiting for Peter outside. Instead there was a police barricade around the entrance and my friends were nowhere in sight.

I saw the policeman who had been in front of Danielle's apartment directing people around the barricade. I ran up to him.

"What's going on?" I asked.

"There's been another death," he said.

"Oh my God," I said, terrified that it was one of my friends. "Who is it?"

"Another one of the Rockettes," he said. "The one named"—he looked down at the paper in his hand—"Nevaeh Anderson."

"What happened to her?" I asked.

"Same as that first Rockette. That Glenna.

She fell into the moving machines under the stage. There's a loose rail there. Nobody ever fixed it after the first time. Nevaeh must have leaned on it and fallen into the gears."

"Do you know where my friends are?" I asked.

"Who are your friends?"

"There are five of us. We're dancing with the Rockettes in their Christmas show. They usually wait out here in front of the theater for someone to pick us up and drive us back to New Jersey."

"Good-looking chicks?" he said. "In a black van?"

"Yes. That's them," I said. "Did you see them?"

"They left just before you got here," he said. "Their van couldn't stay here. We made the driver leave."

I realized I had turned my phone off when I walked the labyrinth. Tina had probably tried to call me. I would have to get a train home. Luckily, Penn Station was only a few blocks away. I started to walk downtown when a familiar voice said, "There you are. I've been looking for you. I've got to talk to you."

It was Andrea and she sounded frantic.

"Andrea!" I said. "I thought you were at the Frick with Tina."

"I was, but when I heard about Nevaeh, I knew I had to tell somebody about Glenna's death before they get me next."

"What do you mean 'they'?" I asked. "Do you know who killed Glenna and Danielle and Nevaeh? And why are you next?"

"Let's go somewhere we can talk," she said.

"Don't you want to talk to the police?" I

asked. "To Detective Carver? If you know who the murderer is, you've got to tell him—not me."

"When I tell you, you'll know why I don't want to go to the police," she said. "Oh please, Mary Louise, I've got to tell you about this. Right away. My time is really short."

I could tell from the expression on her face that she was desperate. I looked around and saw a coffee shop nearby on Sixth Avenue.

"Come on," I said. "Let's go over there."

The coffee shop wasn't too crowded, so we headed for a booth in the back and ordered two coffees. I leaned toward her. "Why did you want to talk to me anyway?" I asked. "How come you didn't confide in Tina? You were right there with her at the Frick."

"Because you helped Danielle and she trusted you, so I trust you too. She was going to tell you about Glenna but was killed before she could do that. I was hoping I'd find you before you left for home."

"Just so you know, Andrea, I will go to the police with anything you tell me about Glenna's murder."

"I do know that. I can't stop you. But I have to tell somebody while I still can."

She lowered her voice so that I could barely hear her. "It was all Marlowe's idea," she said and stopped.

"What idea?" I prodded her.

"To get rid of Glenna," she said. "I just thought she was going to get her fired. I had no idea she meant to kill her or I never would have gone along with the whole crazy scheme."

"Why did she want to do that?" I asked.

"Because she wanted to be the top Rockette herself. She was next in line for it, and she knew Glenna would never give it up. Glenna wasn't that great at the job, actually, so when Marlowe told us that she was going to get her fired and take over the job herself, we were secretly glad she was going to do it. I would have more time at the Frick without Glenna's constant complaining about it. Danielle could keep her baby and her job. And Nevaeh wouldn't have to worry about being fired because she wasn't white. Shelli just got involved because she has a crush on Marlowe and will do anything she says. Marlowe never said anything about killing Glenna at first."

"Why did she tell the four of you what she was going to do?"

"She knew that we all had a reason to wish Glenna was no longer our boss," Andrea said. "She needed our help. When she explained what she wanted us to do, I realized she was talking about killing Glenna, not just getting her fired. I told her I didn't want anything to do with it, to leave me out of it. She said I was already involved because she had told all of us she was going to do it, and if we didn't go to the police we were accomplices."

"Is that true?" I asked.

"I wasn't going to take any chances, so I said I wouldn't tell. I had every intention of going right to the police after she talked to me."

"What about the others?" I asked. "I can't imagine Danielle or Nevaeh helping her with this."

"Danielle and Nevaeh both said what I said—that they wouldn't tell the police."

"But you said Marlowe needed your help, all of you. What did she want you to do?"

Andrea dumped some sugar in her coffee.

"She needed one person to move the time signal ahead that tells the guys who lower the stage when to do it. She easily persuaded Shelli to do that. She also needed someone to get Glenna under the stage on some pretext or other. Somehow she got Danielle to do that."

"Danielle?" I said, surprised. "That nice Danielle? Why would she agree to do that?"

"Danielle wasn't all that crazy about Glenna because Glenna didn't want her to dance while pregnant. Glenna said her pregnancy would show in some of the tight costumes we wore. She told Danielle to either get rid of the baby or quit. Danielle needed the money, and she certainly wasn't going to get rid of the baby after losing the first one. So she went along with Marlowe's plan to get rid of Glenna. I don't think she really understood what Marlowe really had in mind. Or if she did, she blocked it out. I think she still thought Marlowe wanted to get Glenna fired."

"How did Nevaeh get involved?" I asked. "She doesn't seem like the type who would help with anything like this either."

"You're right. She's a good person," Andrea said. "But Glenna was trying to get rid of her and the other three black dancers because she wanted an all-white line of Rockettes. It wasn't really racist. Glenna just liked to have everything match. And Nevaeh didn't match."

"That makes no sense," I said. "The black dancers are great additions to the line. They should have done that years ago. Anyway, go ahead."

"Marlowe told Nevaeh she would never get rid of her or the other black dancers because the Rockettes needed some diversity to be more interesting. She even said that with Glenna gone she would hire more dancers of color. She told Nevaeh all she had to do was call Glenna on her phone while she was under the stage to ask her a question about anything at all and keep her on the phone so Danielle could get out of there before Glenna somehow fell into the machinery under the stage."

"How did Marlowe plan to manage that?"

"She loosened all the screws on the railings above the machinery. When Glenna went over to the rail to confirm that the machinery under the stage was moving before it was supposed to, the rail would give way and she would fall down into the heavy, rotating machines and be killed."

"What was your part in all of this?" I asked.

"She asked me to go to the coffee shop—not this one, down the street from the theater—with her so she wouldn't be in the theater when this happened. I would be her witness. She promised me I could keep working at the Frick as much as I wanted and still dance in the Christmas show. I figured there was always a chance Glenna wouldn't lean against the rail and wouldn't be killed. So, God help me, I agreed to do that. I've tortured myself with it ever since. How could I have agreed to such a thing?"

"I still don't understand why you're telling me all this instead of going to the police," I said.

"Danielle and Nevaeh are dead and I know I'm next," she said. "Marlowe isn't going to let me walk around knowing what I know. I wanted somebody else to know about this in case I'm killed too."

"But you can't just wait around for Marlowe to kill you," I said. "I assume you think Marlowe killed Danielle and Nevaeh to keep them from talking."

"Don't you?"

"It certainly looks that way," I said. "But you've got to go to the police with this information. I mean right away. While you're still alive. And, come to think of it, while I'm still alive."

"I know you're right," she said. "I just don't want to go to jail for the part I played in all this. I'm taking a plane to Canada tonight. I'm a Canadian citizen and I can just disappear there. I know how."

"So you're telling me that all five of you were involved in Glenna's murder?" I asked, still not able to believe this.

"Yes. That's the truth," she said with tears in her eyes. "Are you really going to tell the police?"

"I'm afraid so, Andrea," I said, finishing my coffee. "I'll get you the name of a good New York defense lawyer from George."

I checked the time on my phone and stood up.

"I've got to get a train home," I said. "It's after five thirty and there's a train around six fifteen."

"So you're not going right to the police today?" Andrea asked.

"Not today," I said. "I want to go home. But tomorrow for sure."

"That'll give me a chance to get away," she said. "Thanks, Mary Louise."

I realized I was now an accessory to Glenna's murder by letting Andrea get away, but somehow I couldn't help myself.

"I might still call, Andrea," I said. "I'm going to leave to get my train. Are you getting out of here?"

"In a minute," she said. "Go ahead. They can't kill me here."

I left the cafe and started walking down Sixth Avenue. I'd only gone a block when a van pulled up next to me and the driver honked his horn. It was Peter.

"Mary Louise," he said. "Get in."

"What are you doing here?" I asked, climbing into the back seat of the van with the rest of my friends.

"You didn't think we'd leave without you, did you?" Tina said. "Peter refused to desert you here in the city. He's been circling around looking for you."

"I love you, Peter," I said, leaning over the front seat to kiss him.

"He does have his moments," Tina said. "Where were you all this time?"

"Mike took me to walk a labyrinth down by the East River," I said. "You guys have got to go down there with me. It's the most amazing experience. I walked along that path, and I felt so peaceful when I got to the center. It's incredible."

"Labyrinths are remarkable," Gini said. "When I lived in France, I walked the one in Chartres cathedral that most labyrinths are modeled on. It was unbelievable. I still remember the feeling of total peace when I did that."

"That's how I felt too," I said.

"Have you been down by the river all this time?" Tina asked.

"No, no," I said. "I took a cab back to the theater, but by that time the police were there and they told me you had already left. 'Good-looking chicks' the policeman called you."

"A man of excellent taste," Gini said.

"So what did you do?" Tina asked.

"I started to walk to Penn Station when Andrea popped up and said she had to talk to me, that it was urgent. So I went to a cafe with her and she told me the most amazing story. Wait till you hear this."

I went over the whole murder plot Andrea had described to me.

"They're all in on this?" Gini asked.

"Every one of them," I said. "Danielle and Nevaeh are dead and Andrea is sure she's next."

"In other words, Marlowe is bumping off the others so they won't tell the police?" Gini asked.

"Right," I said. "And Shelli is helping her."

"And now you know too," Gini said. "You'd better hire a bodyguard."

"Marlowe doesn't know I know," I said.

"She knows both Danielle and Nevaeh tried to tell you."

"I'm telling Detective Carver tomorrow," I said.

"You should call him tonight," Peter said. "Seriously, Mary Louise. Call him."

His voice was so insistent, I promised I would.

"What did the rest of you guys do after the rehearsal was canceled?" Peter said, heading for the Lincoln Tunnel.

"I met Tom at Bargemusic," Janice said. "We talked to this really nice woman about our wedding. They usually have classical music concerts there, but it's also the most wonderful place to get married in. Have you ever been on it? It's this old coffee barge remodeled into a romantic place. Wait till you see. It's anchored at the Fulton Ferry landing near the Brooklyn Bridge. We'll have the ceremony there and then go to this great restaurant nearby—the River Cafe—for our reception."

"When are you doing this?" Pat asked.

"Next spring," Janice said. "My daughter Sandy will be my maid of honor."

I knew how much it meant to Janice to have her daughter as her maid of honor because of their troubled relationship in the past. Now they were working on a book together about the Gypsy Robe, a Broadway tradition with a fascinating history. At the opening of every new musical in New York, the robe is passed on to the gypsy—they call the chorus line *gypsies*—who has danced in the most musicals on Broadway. The robe is covered with souvenirs from other shows, like parts of costumes or playbills or photos of other dancers. Half an hour before the show opens, the winner circles the whole group while each gypsy reaches out and touches the robe. It will be a wonderful book, full of the stories from Broadway musicals and great photographs of all the robes.

"It's going to be a beautiful book, Jan," I said. "I'm so glad you're doing it." I asked Gini what she had been up to.

"I went up to Alex's office at the *Times*," Gini said. "He introduced me to a reporter who's going to help me adopt Amalia in India. It won't be easy, but this guy has spent a lot of time in India as a reporter and actually wrote a book about working there. He's familiar with their laws. Alex says he can probably tell me what steps to take to adopt Amalia. Keep your fingers crossed, everybody."

"By the way," Pat said, "when are you and Alex going to follow Janice and Tom's example and get married?"

"I don't know, Pat," Gini said. "We have such a good relationship, it seems a shame to spoil it by getting married."

"Oh, Gini," Pat said. "Not all marriages are like your first one."

"Just kidding," Gini said. "Don't take me so seriously all the time, Pat. Lighten up."

"It's just that you and Alex are such a good

match," Pat said. "I think you'd have a terrific marriage."

"I know," Gini said. "But we have lots of time to think about marriage. Things are really good right now. We don't have to rush into anything. And, not to change the subject, but what did you do this afternoon?"

"Denise and I took David to the Statue of Liberty," Pat said. "We decided that would be more fun than the Circle Line Cruise. I've never been there. That's weird, you know? I've lived here almost all my life, and I've never been to the Statue of Liberty."

"You climbed all those stairs to the top?" Tina asked.

"Yeah, I did," she said. "I thought I was going to die. But I'm so glad I did it. David loved it. He practically ran up those stairs. There's something about being at the top of that statue and looking out at New York from the crown of the statue that symbolizes our freedom that was awesome."

We were quiet, savoring the emotion in Pat's voice as she shared this moment with us.

"David has added so much to my life," she said. "I never would have done that if he wasn't with me today."

We rode the rest of the way back to Champlain in contented silence, once more grateful for the friendship that warmed the five of us.

Peter let me off at my house. I was glad to see that George was already there.

"Hello, Happy Hoofer," he said, kissing me when I opened the door. "How was rehearsal?"

I told him what had happened and about my meeting with Andrea.

"I'm not letting you go back in there without me," he said.

"I'll be all right, George," I said. "I'll be with my friends the whole time. They're not going to let me out of their sight."

"I don't want anything to happen to you," he said. "Today with you in Washington Square was so good."

I smiled at him. "It was perfect," I said. "Like old times."

"Yes, it was," he said. "I'm sorry if I haven't been there for you lately, Mary Louise. Sometimes I just feel overwhelmed."

"I know," I said. "We need to go away for a couple of weeks' vacation after the Alderson case so you can unwind. To Saint Bart's, maybe. Remember what a lovely time we had there?"

"It was great. Or maybe Puerto Vallarta. Our own little villa with a pool."

He put his arms around me. "I love you, Mary Louise."

"I love you too," I said. And I meant it.

> **Mary Louise's cooking tip: If you're looking for a good recipe, *TV Guide* probably isn't the best place to find it.**

Chapter 10

Always Eat A Good Breakfast

"Call that detective—what's his name—?" George said the next morning as I was starting to make breakfast.

"Carver."

"Yeah, Carver. Call him now, please, honey."

"I will, George," I said. "Don't worry. You convinced me. Just let me get breakfast on the table and I'll call him. I promise."

"Okay" he said, sliding the wrapper off *The New York Times*.

He flipped through the paper while I made him his favorite breakfast, my oatmeal and yogurt pancakes that were so good it was hard to believe they were so healthy. I put a glass of orange juice in front of him and he started to take a sip, when he said, "Hey, Mary Louise. There's a story about Nevaeh's death in here. Listen to this. 'A second Rockette, Nevaeh Anderson, has been killed by falling into the machinery under the stage at Radio City Music Hall. The police are conducting an investigation after a loose railing gave way and Ms. Anderson plunged to her death. The first Rockette, Glenna Parsons, died the same way a few days ago.'"

George handed me my cell phone from the counter. "Call. Now. Please, honey."

I put the pancakes in front of him with a pitcher of warmed maple syrup, poured his coffee, and dialed the police department in New York. I had put that number on speed dial after Danielle's death.

"I need to speak to Detective Carver," I said to the officer answering the phone.

"I'm afraid he's not available at the moment," the police officer said.

"This is urgent," I said. "I have crucial information for him about the Radio City deaths."

"I'll have him call you back as soon as possible," she said. "What's your name and what information do you want to give him?"

"Mary Louise Temple. And it's a little complicated. I prefer to talk to him about this," I said.

"It may be a while," the officer said and hung up.

"I'd better go find him—he must be at the theater," I said. "I don't know if there will be a rehearsal or not, but Peter is taking us in there this morning."

"Just don't go near any loose railings," George said taking a forkful of pancakes. "These are great."

I took a couple of bites of my own pancakes and slurped down some coffee.

"I've got to get ready. Peter will be here soon."

I left the kitchen, ran upstairs to brush my teeth, grab my dancing shoes, wrench my hair into a knot in back and come back down for another gulp of coffee before I heard Peter's horn outside.

"Call me after you talk to the detective," George said.

"I will," I said, rescuing my phone from the counter and putting it into my purse.

I got in the car and greeted my half-conscious friends.

RECIPE FOR PANCAKES

Serves 2

3 35-gram packages of instant strawberry
   oatmeal
1 6-oz.container strawberry yogurt
1 large egg
2 t. vanilla
½ t. cinnamon
½ t. nutmeg
¼ cup corn oil
Maple syrup to taste

1. Put the first six ingredients in a food proces-
sor and blend.
2. Heat corn oil in a frying pan.
3. Put a large serving spoonful of batter into the
oil for each pancake you're making. The recipe
makes about six medium-sized pancakes.
4. Turn the pancakes when they are a nice
golden brown on one side.
5. Do the same with the other side of the pancake.
6. Serve with warmed maple syrup.

**Mary Louise's Cooking Tip: If you're making
something that's breaded, use panko. It's
lighter and better than bread crumbs.**

Chapter 11

How About A Circle Line Cruise?

"**A**re you sure there's a rehearsal this
morning?" I asked Tina. "I mean after
Nevaeh's murder or accident or whatever you
want to call it."

"We don't know," Tina said. "But we wanted
to be with you when you tell the detective what
Andrea told you yesterday. We don't want you to
be alone."

"Thanks," I said. "I don't know what I'd do
without you guys."

"We can't let anything happen to you," Gini
said. "You're too good a cook."

Peter pulled up to the theater. We piled out and traipsed into the lobby. Andrea was waiting for us.

"Detective Carver is questioning some of the other Rockettes," she said. "He asked if you would wait for him backstage."

We started toward the stage when Andrea whispered to me, "Can I see you for a second, Mary Louise?"

"What are you doing here, Andrea?" I asked. "I thought you were getting a plane to Canada last night?"

"Something came up, and I had to change my plans. That's what I wanted to talk to you about."

I assumed she was going to tell me something more about the plot to kill Glenna. I motioned for the others to go ahead without me and followed her back to the foyer.

"Don't say a word," she said. "Just walk out to the curb and get into the car that's waiting there."

"But I don't . . ." I started to say and felt something hard against my side under my jacket.

"I have a gun," she said, smiling at one of the guides standing nearby waiting to take another group on a tour of the theater. "Just keep quiet and walk. Don't think I won't use it. I'm in too much trouble myself to worry about you."

I did what she told me. When we got outside to the curb, I saw the car with Shelli in the driver's seat and Marlowe in the passenger seat next to her. Andrea pushed me into the back seat and sat down next to me with her gun pointed at me.

"Good work, Andrea," Marlowe said. "We'll get rid of Miss Muffet, and she won't be able to tell Carver what you told her, and you won't have to go to jail. We'll help you get out of the country."

I looked at Andrea. Andrea, whom I thought was my friend. The one who told me about the whole plot to kill Glenna just yesterday. Andrea, the arranger of weddings at the Frick. I couldn't believe this was happening.

"Andrea . . . what . . . ?"

"Sorry about this, Mary Louise," she said. "It was either you or me. I chose me. I'm leaving the country as soon as we get rid of you."

"Why did you tell me about the murders yesterday if you planned to kill me too?"

"When I talked to you yesterday," she said, "I was planning to head for Canada immediately. I figured you would tell the police and they would arrest Marlowe. But right after you left the coffee shop, Marlowe came in and threatened to kill me if I didn't help her get rid of you. I had no choice."

"You can't possibly get away with this," I said. "My friends will realize something happened to me when I don't come back from talking to you and they'll send the police after you."

"The police have no way of knowing where you are," Marlowe said. "This isn't our car. They don't know what it looks like or what the license plate number is. They're certainly not going to stop a car that has the decal, *A Graduate of Wellesley College* on the back window. No one will know where you are until they find your body."

I looked at Andrea. Was she actually going to

let Marlowe kill me? I couldn't believe it. Her
hand holding the gun was shaking.

"How do you plan to kill me?" I asked Marlowe.

"You'll find out," she said. "Just keep your
mouth shut or we'll do it sooner."

Shelli pulled away from the curb. "Where
to?" she asked Marlowe.

"Get on the West Side Highway going south,"
she said. "Keep on it to Forty-Second Street, and
get off at the Circle Line Cruise pier." She
grinned at me. "How long has it been since you
were on a Circle Line Cruise, honey? Time you
went on another one, don't you think?" She
leaned over the front seat until her face was
close to mine. "Only this time you won't come
back," she said.

I had to think of something, anything, to get
out of this car. Shelli was driving very slowly.
The traffic was heading toward the highway. I
could easily jump out of the car at this speed,
but Andrea would shoot me before I could do
it. I had to think of something else. I decided to
try to distract Marlowe.

"There must be an easier way to kill me than
on the Circle Line Cruise, Marlowe," I said.
"Why did you pick that way?"

Marlowe poked Shelli on the shoulder, still
not taking her eyes off me. "Hurry up. What's
taking you so long?"

"I can't help it," Shelli said. "The traffic is really heavy. Lots of cabs and trucks."

"Well, try to move faster," Marlowe said. She
turned back to me. "Why the Circle Line cruise?

It amuses me. After I shoot you, I'll dump you overboard and get off at the next stop, go back for our car, and show up at the theater, worried because you haven't shown up yet. 'Where could she be?' I'll say, my voice breaking in the middle of the sentence." She laughed that hateful laugh again.

"How are you going to shoot me and throw me in the river with people all around?" I asked to keep her talking, not shooting. "Those cruises are crowded."

"I'll figure that out when we get on board."

Once I got on that ship, I'd think of some way to get away from this crazy woman. No way could she shoot me and toss me in the water on a boat full of tourists.

"This is all fine with you, Andrea?" I said to her.

"I . . . I . . ." she stammered.

Marlowe reached over the front seat and grabbed the gun away from Andrea. "You'll be in the river with her unless you do exactly what I tell you to do," she said to her. "Understand?"

Andrea nodded.

Shelli got on the West Side Highway and took the next exit ramp to Forty-Second Street. She drove to the pier where the Circle Line Cruise docked, then parked the car and waited for instructions from Marlowe.

Marlowe reached in the glove compartment and took out another gun and handed it to Shelli.

"You cover the fake Rockette, and I'll walk with Andrea to make sure she doesn't try anything funny. I already have the tickets, so we'll act like tourists and get on the boat."

I felt pressure against my foot. Andrea was trying to send me a message. I glanced at her when Marlowe looked away for a minute to talk to Shelli. Andrea motioned with her head for me to look down at the floor. She had dropped her iPhone there with a text message on it. I just had time to read **Do what I do**, before Marlowe looked back. Andrea had already slid her phone into her pocket. She was on my side. Somehow we would get out of this together, please God.

Shelli opened the door on my side of the car and told me to get out. She put her arm around my waist and I could feel the gun against my side under my jacket. Marlowe opened the door on Andrea's side and motioned to her to get out. She took her arm and said, "Don't try anything or you're dead."

I knew there was no way either of them could shoot us in the middle of the crowd of people boarding the boat, and I was sure Andrea knew that too. I waited to get some kind of signal from her as we walked up the ramp going onto the boat. Andrea and Marlowe were ahead of Shelli and me. Halfway up the ramp that had no rails on the side, Andrea shouted, "*Now*," and shoved Marlowe with all her might into the water. I did the same thing to Shelli who fell off the ramp on the other side.

Andrea grabbed my hand and said, "Run!" She pulled me down the ramp, pushing the other tourists aside until we reached the pier.

There were cabs parked nearby and we jumped in one.

"Quick," Andrea said. "Get us to the Music Hall as fast as you can."

"Must be good movie there," the driver said with a heavy Russian accent. "What is?"

"Just drive. Hurry," Andrea said.

The driver maneuvered around the other cabs and headed east toward Sixth Avenue.

My heart was pounding so hard I thought I would pass out.

"Are you all right?" Andrea asked.

"I don't know," I said. "I'm totally confused. Whose side are you on anyway? I thought you were going to help her kill me."

"I thought so too," she said. "Then in the car, I realized she was planning to kill me on that boat too. She couldn't let me stay alive knowing what I knew, so I made up my mind to get both of us away from her."

"She'll probably still try to get us," I said.

"It'll take her and Shelli a while to climb out of that river and dry off," Andrea said. "We'll be safe in the theater with Detective Carver, telling him what happened."

"Aren't you still afraid of going to jail?" I asked.

"I can't run away any more," she said. "I didn't really do anything except go to a cafe with her. And I certainly wasn't going to watch while she killed you."

"Thank God for that," I said.

The cab driver got us to the theater in about

ten minutes and we ran inside. I prayed that the detective would still be there.

He was. "What happened to you?" he said to me when we climbed onto the stage.

My friends surrounded us. "Where were you?" Tina asked. "When you didn't come back, we went looking for you and you had disappeared."

I told them what had happened and emphasized what Andrea had done to save my life.

"But you have to get them," I said to the detective, grabbing his arm. "They're probably just being pulled out of the water. You have to get them before they drive away. They have a car down there."

Detective Carver barked orders into his phone to his men to proceed immediately to the Circle Line pier and arrest two soaking-wet women in the boarding area.

"They can't get away," he said to me.

A few minutes later, I noticed that Detective Carver was talking on his phone again with a worried look on his face. Uh-oh. *Please don't let him say what I know he's going to say.*

When he hung up, he still had the same look.

"Detective?" I said, afraid to ask him.

"Ms. Temple, I'm afraid I have bad news," he said.

"They got away, didn't they?" I asked.

"Yes. I can't imagine how they got out of there, soaking wet, police all over the dock looking for them."

"They had a car parked on the dock, Detective. They might have gotten away in that."

"A car?" the Detective said. "What did it look like?"

"They got us out of there so fast I didn't get much chance to look at the plate," I said. "It wasn't a New York plate. But the car is a beige Nissan sedan. Not a new one. At least five years old, I think. The seats inside are black. I'm afraid that isn't much help. There must be a thousand cars like that on the road."

"We'll check the dock first," he said. "They might not have made it to the car. It could still be there. Do you remember anything else about it? Anything at all?"

Then I remembered something. "Oh there is one thing. The back window had *A Graduate of Wellesley College* printed on it."

"That's it!" he said. He got back on his phone and told the officer on the other end to check the dock for a car like the one I had described to him. "Did she tell you who the graduate was?" he asked me.

"No. She just said it wasn't her car. She must have stolen it from the Radio City garage. I don't think Wellesley accepts potential murderers."

He gave a quick bark of a laugh. "That's a huge help," he said.

The detective clicked on his cell phone again. "Get me the guy who runs the garage in Radio City Music Hall," he said. After a minute, he continued. "Mr. Spinella? This is Detective Carver. Have there been any reports of stolen cars in the last few days?" He listened then said, "Will you notify me if anyone reports a stolen car, please? It's very important. We're looking for a beige Nissan with the words *A Graduate of Wellesley College* on the back window. Sound familiar?" He listened some more and his face changed. "That's extremely helpful, Mr. Spinella. Thank you. Do you have a license number for that car?"

He waited a few more minutes, scribbled something down in a notebook, thanked the garage manager, and hung up. Then he spoke to me, the excitement of what he just heard reflected in his voice.

"No wonder nobody reported a stolen car," he said. "It belonged to Nevaeh Anderson! She kept it parked in the Radio City garage all the time. She didn't have to pay because she was a Rockette. So nobody reported it when it disappeared. They just assumed she had taken it out for some reason. Even after she was killed, they didn't think to report her car as stolen. Marlowe took it. Now we have a license number. We'll get them if they managed to get to the car and drive away. If they didn't get to the car, they should be easy to find walking around in wet clothes near the dock."

I wasn't so sure of that. Marlowe was a pretty slippery character. If anyone could escape from that dock, sopping wet or not, she could. And she'd drag that nitwit Shelli along with her. I so wanted to believe Detective Carver.

"I'll call you as soon as we get their car and arrest them," the detective said. "I know you're scared. I don't blame you. You had a really bad experience."

"Please call me as soon as you catch them, Detective," I said.

I knew I wouldn't feel completely safe until those two were in jail for the rest of their lives. But for now, I was supposed to dance in that fat suit.

"What do we do now?" I asked Tina. "There's nobody left to rehearse us. Are we still going to be in that Christmas show?"

"We have you to show us what to do, Andrea. Right?" Tina said.

"I'm afraid not, Tina," Andrea said. "I'm in the middle of this whole mess."

"As a matter of fact," the detective said, "my men are waiting to take you to headquarters right now." He motioned to two of his police officers standing on the side of the stage. They came forward to handcuff Andrea and take her downtown.

"Could I just say something before you take her?" I said to Detective Carver.

"Of course, Ms. Temple," he said. "What is it?"

"If it weren't for Andrea, I'd be lying at the bottom of the river with a bullet in my head." I told him again what she had done to save my life.

"I'm sure they'll take that into account," he said. "But right now, she's got a lot to answer for."

My mind flashed back to Andrea holding a gun against my side when we left the theater. I wasn't going to argue with him.

He nodded to the policemen who took Andrea down the aisle and out of the theater.

* * *

Tina looked around at all of us. "What do you say, gang? Do we stay or quit and go home?"

"Please, let's quit, Tina." Pat said. I've had enough of people being mangled in machinery and heavy Santa outfits and perfect Rockettes."

"I'm with Pat," Janice said. "We usually have so much fun on these jobs, but this one has been a nightmare from beginning to end."

"We can't quit, guys," Gini said. "If we do, we're leaving the Rockettes without any comic relief and they need something extra with five of their best dancers gone. There's nobody to help them put a little life into the show. We owe them that, don't we? It's only for a couple of months."

"I think we should let Mary Louise decide," Tina said. "She's the one who's been through the worst of all this. Do you want to quit, Weez?"

"I was going to say yes, yes, yes," I said. "Having a gun pointed at me is not fun. But I think Gini is right. We can't desert all those other Rockettes now. They must be totally demoralized. Let's stick it out. The only thing I would ask is that they get rid of those heavy Santa jackets. They're horrible to dance in. Ask whoever is in charge now to give us lighter costumes."

"If Weezie can stay after what she's gone through, I think the rest of us can too," Tina said. "Pat? Janice?"

My friends both agreed and Tina went off to find the person in charge to tell her we were staying.

> **Mary Louise's cooking tip:** Make some delicious little cheese puffs to go with that bottle of champagne.

Chapter 12

Cruising At Sunset

My friends surrounded me.

"We're not going anywhere without you until the police arrest Marlowe and Shelli," Gini said.

"That's right," Tina said, coming back on stage.

"Did you find somebody to tell that we're staying" Gini asked her.

"Yes, there's a very nice woman named Bianca in charge now," Tina said. "She was so relieved to hear that we're going to be in the show. She's overwhelmed, and I felt she really needed us."

"What do we do now?" Janice asked.

"Wait till you hear," Tina said. "I called Peter a minute ago, and when he heard what happened to our little buttercup here, he insisted on coming to get us."

"Doesn't that man ever work?" Gini asked.

"He's a partner in his law firm, Gini," Tina said. "He sets his own hours. He had the best idea."

"Tell us," Janice said.

Tina could hardly contain herself. "He's going to come and get us and drive over to Chelsea Piers, where his boat is anchored. He's going to take us on a sunset cruise around Manhattan—with champagne! His boat is gorgeous."

"I should probably get back home to George," I said. "He'll be worried if I don't show up. I promised him I'd be there to make dinner."

"Not to worry, Weez," Tina said. "Peter said he would call George and have him meet us on the boat. He's also calling Alex, Tom, Denise, and David to come sailing with us."

Everybody talked at once, thanking Tina, making their own phone calls, generally jumping up and down with delight.

"You'd better marry that man before he gets away," Gini said. "I always liked him, but I didn't know he had his own boat!"

"He doesn't talk about the things he owns very much," Tina said. "He thinks that's crass."

I was so glad my best friend was going to marry this practically perfect man.

"Okay, everyone," Tina said, clapping her hands together. "Let's go out front and wait for our hero."

Pat put her arm around me. "Are you going to be okay, Mary Louise? You've just been through hell. Do you want to do this?"

I'm always grateful for Pat's kindness and insight. She knew I wasn't really back to normal after being held at gunpoint and told I was going to be shot and thrown in the river. It's not the kind of thing you get over right away. But the more I thought about it and felt the warmth and love of my four friends, the more I welcomed the idea of a boat ride at sunset around my beloved Manhattan

"I'm getting there, Pat," I said. "You're an angel to worry about me. I think this is just the thing to help me get over this horrible day."

We followed Tina out of the theater, and before long, Peter's van pulled up to the curb. An officer got out of one of the police cars parked nearby and approached Peter.

"Excuse me, sir," he said. "We're keeping this area cordoned off. I'm afraid you can't park here."

"It's all right, Sergeant," Detective Carver said. He had followed us out of the theater. "These people are leaving right away."

"Thank you, Detective," Tina said. "We are so grateful to you."

"Don't worry," Carver said. "We'll get them."

He turned to me and put his hand on my shoulder. "I'm sorry you had to go through that today," he said. "Are you all right?"

What a kind man, I thought. No wonder that little kitty cat Ranger took to him right away.

"I'll be fine, Detective," I said. "Thank you for your concern."

Carver motioned for one of his officers to open the door of Peter's car, and we all jumped in, ready for champagne and caviar and a sunset cruise.

I kissed Peter on top of his head when I got in the car. "You're absolutely the very best person on earth to do this, Peter. I need it so badly."

"I figured you might," he said. "You've been through hell today."

He started the van. "Ready for a boat ride, ladies?" he said.

A loud chorus of *yays* and *hurrahs* and *you bets* made him laugh, and he headed west toward Chelsea Piers, where his boat was anchored.

"Were you able to get in touch with everybody?" Tina asked Peter.

"I was. They were all really excited, and they're going to meet us at the dock."

"Even George?" I asked. "He's coming all the way from New Jersey?"

"Luckily he was in the city again to talk to that witness of his. I told him what happened to you today, and he said to look after you until he got there."

It took us about twenty minutes to get to the pier, where Peter parked near a sleek white yacht moored there.

"There she is," Peter said.

The first thing I noticed was the name on the boat: Dancer. What could be more perfect?

"How did you ever come up with a name like that for your boat, Peter?" I asked, teasing him.

"I wonder," he said, leaning over to give Tina a kiss on the cheek. The way she looked at him, I knew they would have a long and happy life together.

Peter got out of the car and opened the doors for us. "Careful on that ramp, Hoofers," he said. "Can't have anyone falling in . . ." Tina punched him and he remembered what had happened to me that morning. "Oh, sorry, Weezie," he said.

"It's all right, Peter," I said. "I'm heading for that champagne."

When I walked into the main salon of Peter's yacht, I was overwhelmed by its beauty. All the couches and chairs were white leather. The bar and end tables were mahogany. There were flowers everywhere. An Asian man with a friendly smile came forward to greet us.

"This is Andre, everybody," Peter said. "He does everything on this boat. I just drive it but he does everything else."

We could see champagne bottles chilling in buckets on the side, with glasses next to them. There were platters of caviar, pâté, little yummy-looking hors d'oeuvres, and of course, Peter being Peter, there was a bottle of non-alcoholic wine for Pat and David. It was bubbly and looked just like champagne.

"As soon as the rest of our group gets here, we'll take off," Peter said. "In the meantime, Andre will pour you some champagne."

The events of that morning were already beginning to fade, or at least the horror of it.

Before long, our partners began arriving, all of them obviously delighted to be on this beautiful boat, all of them showing concern for me. Denise and David were the first to arrive. David came over to me right away.

"Were you really almost shot?" David asked.

"I'm afraid I was, David," I said. "But I'm okay now that you're here."

He still looked worried. "There aren't any guns on this boat, are there?"

I pulled him to me and gave him a hug. "Not a gun anywhere. Don't worry. Get some fake champagne over there and something to eat. We'll be sailing out into the river pretty soon."

He went over to the table, where Andre poured him a drink.

Denise was embarrassed. "Oh Mary Louise, I didn't mean for David to—."

I hugged her too. "It's all right, Denise. He was just worried about me. He's the sweetest boy."

She looked relieved and joined David to get a glass of fake champagne. Since she and David moved in with Pat, Denise rarely drank anything alcoholic. That made it much easier for Pat, who hadn't had a real drink in a couple of years.

There was a loud clatter as George ran over the ramp and into the room. He walked over to me and took me in his arms and held on to me as if I might disappear any minute.

"She had a gun!" he said. "You were almost shot? Are you all right? Did they catch her?"

"Almost," I said. "Detective Carver was sure they would get her soon."

"You mean she's still out there?" George said.

"She can't get me now, George," I said. "Don't worry."

Andre handed us both a glass of champagne and pointed at the couch nearby. "You would like to sit down?" he asked.

George, still holding onto me tightly, pulled me down on the couch.

"I'm all right, George," I said. "They have the license number of their car. She's probably in jail already."

"Don't worry," David said, coming over to George. "There are no guns on this boat."

George shook David's hand. "That's good to hear," he said. "You must be David. I've heard lots of good things about you."

"Like what?" David asked.

"That you take good care of our Pat and your mom."

David beamed. "Aunt Pat's my mom now too," he said.

Denise came over and said hello to George and led David over to Pat, who was greeting Alex who had just bounced onto the boat. He came over to the couch and knelt in front of me.

"I hear you're trying to get on the front page of *The New York Times*, Weez," he said. "Are you all right?"

"Hello, Alex," I said. "I'm getting there. She probably couldn't have shot me on a Circle Line Cruise anyway. Somebody would have noticed."

"Aren't we going on a Circle Line Cruise tomorrow, Aunt Pat?" David asked, that worried look coming back on his face.

"Maybe we'll go to Governor's Island instead," Pat said.

"What's there?" David asked.

"Sculpture you can climb on and jump over," Pat said. "They call it interactive sculpture, and it's really fun."

"That sounds better than a cruise with guns on it," David said.

"I assume they got her," Alex said to me.

"Not yet," I said. "But I'm sure they'll get her any minute. The police have the license number of the car they're driving."

Alex saw the look on George's face and didn't ask any more questions. Obviously, he wasn't any more sure than I was that they would get her.

"George," Alex said, "you're sailing with us? I didn't think you ever left New Jersey."

"Oh yeah," George said. "Every once in a while I leave our beautiful Garden State to come to your dirty old city."

"I'm glad you're here," Alex said. "We all wanted to be with our Weezie."

"Thanks Alex," George said and held me even more tightly.

Just then Tom came on board and stood looking at the impressive living room for a minute before he said anything.

"Wow," he said. "This is incredible. So this is how the other half lives. Not bad, Peter."

"Hey, Tom," Peter said. "Glad you could come. We all wanted to be with our Mary Louise tonight. We wouldn't be complete without you."

Tom suddenly remembered why we were doing this, and came over to me on the couch. "Are you okay, Weez?" he asked.

"I'm fine, Tom," I said. "Now that you're on board."

He gave me a kiss on the forehead and joined Janice at the champagne table.

"If we're all here, I'll take us out onto the river," Peter said. "The sun is just starting to go down, so you'll see our city at its loveliest."

He went to the front of the boat and steered the yacht out into the Hudson River. We all quieted down and marveled at this wondrous city as we sailed slowly by. The Chrysler Building and the Empire State Building to the north stood out against the sky. We passed the new memorial to the World Trade Center standing brave and tall in lower Manhattan.

The sky was turning red and yellow and orange as we approached the Statue of Liberty. Peter slowed the boat down so that it almost stopped at this monument that welcomed people of all colors and races to our shores. We watched the sun slowly sink down behind her. There was almost total quiet on the boat as we were all reminded of how lucky we were to have been born in this country. I noticed that Andre bowed his head and closed his eyes in prayer for a minute.

When the sky was dark, Peter continued on around the tip of the island, past the lights of the restaurants in Battery Park, past the ferry to Staten Island, crowded with commuters going back home, past the boat waiting to go to Governors' Island, then under the Brooklyn Bridge. Soft music played from the speakers in the living room as we took this magical trip. I was almost my normal, unjittery self again by the time Peter turned the yacht around and headed back to the pier at Twenty-Second Street.

It was rare for the five of us Hoofers to be quiet for so long, but I was grateful for the silence. It was restorative, healing, just what I needed.

George held onto me the whole time, as entranced as I was by this lovely trip around the tip of Manhattan. It was a whole new view of this fascinating city.

When we got back to Chelsea Piers, we were still quiet of mind and tongue. We thanked Peter for this ride we would never forget.

"Feel better, Mary Louise?" Peter asked.

"Much better," I assured him. "I can't thank you enough, Peter. This was perfect."

The rest of my friends decided to stay in the city for dinner, but I just wanted to be home, safe with George. He had driven into the city so his car was parked near the boat. We said good-bye to all those dear friends and went back to Champlain.

Mary Louise's cooking tip: Unless you have a cholesterol problem, use butter in your cooking, not that low-fat margarine!

Chapter 13

Ayuda!

I must have slept for ten hours. I woke up the next day refreshed and glad I didn't have to go into the city and put on one of those heavy Santa Claus jackets. It was Saturday. French toast day. I put the bacon in the pan, and it was just beginning to sizzle when the phone rang. *Must be somebody trying to sell me something*, I thought. But the name on my phone was Tina's.

"Tina," I said, "it's Saturday. What are you doing up and on the phone?"

"Hi, Weezie," she said. "I'm so sorry to do this to you, but Bianca—you know, the Rockette who is in charge now—just called me. She's frantic. She asked if we could possibly come into the city and rehearse with the Rockettes today. Without the five main dancers, she's had to change everything around, and she wants to check and see where our dancing will fit in best. I know it's asking a lot, but I told her I'd ask you guys."

"Oh, Tina," I said, "the last thing I want to do is go back in that city on a Saturday and put on that heavy, awful jacket and dance without any-one to direct us."

"I know, hon," she said. "But she needs our help. She's in a real mess, and I think we should help her out. I'll see if I can persuade her to take those heavy balls out of the jackets."

"Two more months before we finish there, Tina," I said.

"Listen," she said. "Think about it: I called the others and they're, reluctantly, going to come into the city with me today. Peter begged off. He loves us, but he doesn't feel like driving in. I'm going to drive, though. I borrowed his van."

"If you're all going, I'll come too," I said. "When?"

"I'll pick you up in an hour," she said. "Okay?"

"I guess," I said.

"Thanks, Weezie," she said. "I know how hard this is for you. I really appreciate it."

"See you in an hour," I said.

George came into the kitchen just as I said that.

"See who in an hour?" he asked.

"Oh, George, I told Tina I'd go into the city with them because the woman in charge of the Christmas show really needs us since she lost all those Rockettes."

"I thought we were going to see that movie— the one with George Clooney you wanted to see," George said.

"So did I," I said. "Believe me, honey, I don't want to do this. But I can't let my friends down."

I put a plate full of crisp bacon and golden brown French toast next to the pitcher of warm maple syrup in front of him and poured a cup of fresh, hot coffee to go with it."

He sighed. "I know I can't stop you, but I wish you wouldn't go."

"Thanks for understanding, honey," I said. "I feel I have to go with the others this morning."

"I know," he said. "It's one of the reasons I love you: your loyalty."

I went upstairs to get dressed and was ready with my tap shoes when Tina drove into the driveway.

Nobody looked very happy. They all sort of grunted a hello when I got in the car, and we didn't say much on the way into the city. Tina made it in record time, since it wasn't a work morning, and parked near the Music Hall.

Bianca was waiting for us on the stage when we came in. She had pulled-back white-blond hair, and the usual red cheeks and pink lipsticked mouth. The customary cheerful Rockettes expression was missing.

"Thank you so much for doing this," she said to us as we climbed onto the stage. "I'm so sorry to have to ask you to do this, but I don't know what else to do. We have this big hole in our line of dancers, and we need you to fill at least a small part of it. After all the bad publicity about the murders, you guys will add some comic relief to this whole Christmas show."

"We still need a lot of rehearsing, Bianca," Tina said. "We kept getting interrupted by people being killed." She paused and looked briefly at me. "Have the police arrested Marlowe and Shelli yet?"

"I don't think so," Bianca said. "But they may have caught them and not told me yet."

"I don't see how they can get away," Tina said.

I did. Marlowe always found a way to do what she had to do. And getting rid of me was at the top of her list.

"Okay," Bianca said, "if you're ready, here are the Santa jackets to put on."

We all groaned and pulled the heavy costumes over our heads.

"There is one favor you could do for us, Bianca," Tina said. "Take the lead out of these jackets. It would make it so much easier for us."

"I think we could manage that," Bianca said. "Do the best you can today and I'll make sure they're lighter from now on."

Bianca put us through our paces for an hour. It was a little easier than it had been before, but still not a lot of fun.

"Why don't you go get some lunch, and we'll do some more this afternoon," Bianca said. "One of the other Rockettes will take over for me on Monday."

She left and my friends took out their phones to make plans for lunch.

"Wait a minute," Janice said. "We can't leave Mary Louise by herself when Marlowe is still roaming around out there."

"You're right," Gini said. "You can come with us, Weez. Alex and I are eating at The *Times*."

"Oh, Gini," I said, "you don't have to do that. Go have fun with Alex. I'll call Mike. He'll be sure I'm safe."

"Are you still seeing him?" Pat asked. "I got the impression that you had decided to stay with George. You certainly seemed like it on the boat."

"You're right, Pat," I said. "I am going to stay with George, but I'll always have Mike as a friend."

"That's okay with George?" Gini asked, her expression saying just the opposite.

"We'll see," I said. "If he can't handle that, I'll break off my friendship with Mike, but today I want to be with Mike. I want to tell him."

"If you're sure," Tina said. "We don't want to lose you, Weezie." She gave me a hug.

"Let me call him and make sure he's not delivering a baby or something," I said. "And then you can leave me. I'll be fine."

Mike answered his phone right away, the way he always does in case one of his patients is in labor. When I told him what had happened, he said, "Stay there. I'll come get you."

"Thanks, Mike," I said and hung up.

"He's on his way over here," I said to my friends.

"You can go. He'll stay with me until you're ready to take us home, Tina."

"I don't feel right about leaving you here alone, Mary Louise."

"It's all right, Tina," I said. "Mike will be here before I finish dressing. Go ahead. I'll be fine."

"If you're sure," Tina said. "I'm going to talk to the caterer for the wedding, and I'll meet you back here at two.

Janice went off to meet Tom, Gini to meet Alex, and Pat to meet David at Rockefeller Center, where they were going to ice skate. I went into the art deco bathroom to put on some lipstick and comb my hair before Mike got there.

I smoothed my hair back into a reasonably straight look and was putting on my lipstick when the door of one of the booths opened and Marlowe came out, a blond wig on her head, a gun in her hand. She was wearing a sweater and skirt.

I dropped my lipstick in the sink. "Marlowe! How did you get in here? How did you get out of the river? Where's Shelli?"

"You ask too many questions, you little fink. You're not going to get away from me this time. You're my hostage until I get out of this country. If you do what I say, you might live to dance another day."

"How did you get out of the water?" I said, trying to stall until Mike got out of his car and came into the theater to find me.

"Not that it's any of your business, but I'm a good swimmer. It's my favorite kind of exercise. I swam under the dock until I was a long way from the pier where your friend shoved me in the river—thanks a lot—and came up near a restaurant on the water. I used the dryer in the ladies' room until I was respectable again, went to a boutique nearby, bought a wig, a sweater and skirt. I went back to the dock to get our car, but the police must have taken it away. So I came here to wait for you. You won't get away from me this time."

"What happened to Shelli?" I asked.

"I have no idea," she said. "I wasn't going to hang around and find out. Maybe she drowned. Anyway she's history. Now walk out that door. I'm right behind you. And this gun is loaded."

"Where are we going?"

"To the pier. I'm getting a boat to Cuba. I have relatives there. It's owned by a friend of mine. I had a score to settle with you first, though. You're my hostage until that boat sails. I didn't want to take a chance on being arrested while I waited for the boat to leave."

"You have Cuban relatives?" I asked, surprised. Her name was so un-Spanish.

She laughed when she saw my expression. "Marlowe Stanley is my professional name. My grandfather came here when Castro took over Cuba. My real name is Magalys Moreno. Now shut up and don't try anything. Walk."

We went out the back way and she held the gun against my back under my jacket. We looked like very close girlfriends. We had gone about three blocks south on Sixth Avenue when I saw Mike's car coming up Sixth Avenue toward us. I didn't think Marlowe saw him. I had to figure out a way to attract Mike's attention without getting shot.

His car stopped at a red light just as we were about to pass him. I bent down, grabbed one of my shoes and threw it as hard as I could at his windshield before Marlowe could stop me.

He shouted, "Hey," and then realized it was me. He jumped out of the car and ran to us.

"Don't make a move or she's dead," Marlowe said.

"She has a gun, Mike," I said.

Mike stepped back. Meanwhile, all the cars behind Mike's started honking their horns the way drivers do in New York when they can't move. A policewoman approached his car, realized no one was behind the wheel and shouted, "Whose car is this?"

"Better go get your car, Doc," Marlowe said and pulled me along the sidewalk away from him.

Mike ran over to the traffic officer and pointed to Marlowe and me walking down the street. The officer kept talking and motioned toward Mike's car. She didn't seem interested in me, Marlowe, the gun, or anything but removing Mike's car from the intersection where he was blocking traffic.

I had to do something. At the next block, the light turned red as we were about to cross, but I didn't stop walking. I kept going as the cars moved toward us from the right. Marlowe tried to stop me but I just kept on, with the cars squealing to a stop or honking or the drivers shouting at me to get out of the way. I figured I would either get killed by a car or by Marlowe but I didn't really think she would shoot me in the middle of Thirty-Seventh Street.

She still had the gun in my back as she tried to push me across the street to get away from the cars coming at us. A truck driver leaned out of his cab and said, "Hey lady, you're crossing against the light. Do you want to get killed?"

I yelled back at him, "She's got a gun."

"A gun?" the driver said. "Just to cross the street? New York isn't that bad." And he laughed. He had no idea I was serious, that I was walking down Sixth Avenue with a gun in my ribs.

With all the noise and honking and shouting, Marlowe was distracted just long enough for Mike to come up behind her and knock the gun out of her hand, pick it up and point it at her.

Finally, the traffic officer realized what was happening and stopped concentrating on Mike's car in the intersection and understood something far more serious was going on. Unfortunately, she assumed Mike was the criminal, since he was armed, and Marlowe was the victim.

"Okay, Mister," she said, coming up to him, her own gun pointing at him, "drop the gun."

"Oh, thank you, Officer," Marlowe said. "You saved my life. This man was trying to rob me—right in the middle of the street."

"Don't believe her, Officer," I said. "She was kidnapping me, and this man—he's a doctor at New York Hospital—is my friend and was rescuing me."

"You're all under arrest," she said, picking up Marlowe's gun from the sidewalk where Mike had dropped it.

"You have to believe me," I said. "Call Detective Carver. He's after this woman. Her name is Marlowe—"

"You know Detective Carver?" the officer said.

"Call him. My name is Mary Louise Temple. This woman has killed three people. Three Rockettes. Detective Carver has been trying to get her. You'll be a big hero."

"Do you really believe all this stuff this crazy woman is saying," Marlowe said. "Look at her. You can tell she's out of her mind. Do I look as if I could have killed three women? She's nuts."

"She's not crazy," Mike said. "She's telling you the truth. One call to Detective Carver and you'll see. You'll be a hero."

The officer looked from one to the other of us, not sure which one of us was crazy. Finally, she clicked a number on her phone. After a minute she was transferred.

"Detective Carver?" she said. "I don't mean to disturb you, sir, but I'm in the middle of a very confusing situation. A woman named Mary Louise Temple told me to call you. She says she was kidnapped by this woman who's with her. There's some man here too, who says he's a doctor."

She almost dropped the phone because of the explosion of sound at the other end. The detective yelled at her to arrest the other woman immediately. She was wanted for murder. The officer hung up, handcuffed Marlowe and hailed a passing police car with two police officers inside. She explained the situation briefly to them and told them to take her to headquarters. Not to let her out of their sight.

I don't think I have ever been as scared as I was during that whole encounter with Marlowe. I couldn't believe I was still alive and not on a boat on my way to Cuba.

Mike held me close. "Are you all right?"

"No, and I don't think I ever will be all right," I said clinging to him. "Oh, Mike, I'm so glad to see you."

He helped me into his car and started the engine.

"It's all over, honey," he said. "She'll never get out of jail. You're safe."

I didn't believe him.

Mary Louise's cooking tip: No matter what happens to you in life, don't forget to ask for the recipe for whatever you were eating at the time.

Chapter 14

A Hoofer's Prayer

"**A**re you hungry, babe?" Mike asked me. "Want some lunch?"

"I'm not hungry, but I could use a cup of coffee," I said. "And I want to talk to you, Mike. About us."

He didn't say anything, but the expression on his face told me he knew what I was going to tell him.

"There's a cafe nearby," he said. "We can talk there."

Luckily, there was a parking space near the café, and I limped into the restaurant with him. I never did find the shoe I threw at his car, so I hobbled around, his hand on my arm supporting me.

We sat down, ordered coffee, and I looked at this man who meant so much to me.

"Mike," I began. "I—"

"I know, Mary Louise," he said. "I know what you're going to say. I just don't want to hear it." There were tears in his eyes.

"Oh, Mike," I said, holding his hand. "You mean so much to me. I can't tell you how much. I do love you, but I love George too. I'm going to stay with him, but I was hoping you and I could still be friends. I don't want to lose you as a friend."

His smile was sad. "Of course we can still be friends," he said. "But I'll never stop hoping you'll change your mind. I'll always be here for you—especially when someone is trying to murder you."

I shuddered. "It seems to be happening a lot lately," I said.

"I don't know anyone else who needs me for that reason," he said. "Most people I know live ordinary lives with nobody trying to kill them. With you, every day it's a possibility."

"I can't keep you a secret from George any longer, Mike," I said. "It's not fair to him. I'll tell him about you and that I want to see you as a friend. If he can't handle that, then . . ."

"I know," he said. "Then we can't see each other any more. I'll just have to learn to accept that. Unless someone else tries to kill you. Then please feel free to call."

"I'm staying home in Champlain, where as far as I know, there are no murderers," I said. I took his hand. "Thank you for being so understanding, Mike."

"Your honesty is one of the things I love best about you," he said. "I know how hard it has been for you trying to decide what to do." He paused and held my hand in both of his. "I don't know what I'll do without you, though."

"Let's see what George says," I said, knowing he wouldn't exactly be thrilled if I kept on seeing a man who loved me and wanted to marry me.

"I know what I'd say if my wife told me another man was in love with her," Mike said.

His phone vibrated. He took it out of his pocket and listened.

"How far apart are they?" he asked. "I'll be right there." He took my hand. "Will you be all right if I leave you here? There's a new life coming into the world."

I smiled. I loved the way he looked forward to each new baby born with his help. "Of course, Mike. Go welcome that baby."

He stood up and leaned over and kissed me. "Let me know what George says," he said. "Just remember, I love you."

"I know," I said. "Good-bye, Mike." I hoped this wasn't the last time I would ever see him.

He touched my face and hurried out of the restaurant. That baby was on its way.

I sat there, thinking about almost being killed twice in one day and how lucky I was to be alive. I decided to find a church nearby and say a prayer of thanks for escaping from Marlowe. I still had time before I had to go back to the theater and rehearse.

I left some money on the table and walked out of the cafe. There was a small church a block away and I headed for it. It was a Presbyterian church, old and small, with a sign outside saying that the sermon on Sunday would be "Are You Leading the Life God Meant You to Lead?"

I couldn't help but think *Oh, I hope not.* Surely God didn't mean for me to have a gun stuck in my side almost every day.

The church was open. I walked into the quiet darkness that always gave me a feeling of serenity that was missing in the rest of the world. I went to the front of the church and sat down in one of the pews. The altar was a simple one, without the gold and glitter of some of the other sects.

I bowed my head and said a silent *thank you* to God for saving my life, for George's love, for my children who were good, kind people, for my Hoofer friends who were always there for me, and for Mike who loved me no matter what. All in all, I felt I led a good life, and I told God that.

Then I felt somebody move into the pew beside me. *Please let it be one of my friends,* I thought, knowing it probably wasn't. It was just intuition. Then I felt the all too familiar hard end of a gun against my ribs.

I opened my eyes.

"I almost drowned back there when you

shoved me in the water, you rotten bitch," Shelli said. "I can't swim. Now you're gonna get yours."

"Shelli," I said. "Put the gun away. I'll help you. There's a boat leaving for Cuba. Marlowe is on it and she'll take you with her. One of her relatives owns the ship."

"How do you know all that?" Shelli asked, suspicion in her voice and on her face.

"She was going to take me with her, but I got away."

"I don't want to go to Cuba," Shelli said. "I want to get back to Ohio where my sister lives. She'll take care of me. I need you as my hostage until I get there."

This was beginning to get a little repetitious. *I could use a little help here, God,* I said to him silently, hoping He was still listening to me. Shelli wasn't all that bright. I knew I could persuade her to get on the boat going to Cuba. It would just take a little more lying.

"You won't be safe in Ohio, Shelli," I said. "The police will find you there and arrest you. If you go to Cuba with Marlowe, you'll have a good life, safe from American police, living near the beach with your friend."

She looked away from me, considering what I said. Her hand holding the gun moved away from my side and rested on the seat next to her. *Easy now. Just a little more and you've got her.*

"Tell you what," I said. "There's an ATM machine down the block. I passed it before. I'll take out some money for you. How about a thousand dollars? Then you'll have plenty of money when you get to Cuba. I hear it's a beautiful place."

She looked at me, wanting to believe that I was going to help her.

"Well, maybe . . ." she said.

I knocked the gun out of her hand. It fell to the ground and went off. The sound of a gunshot brought the minister out of his office in the back.

"What's going on here?" he shouted.

Shelli ran toward the door and was out of the church before he could stop her.

The minister came over to me, his face contorted and angry. He picked up the gun from the floor and said, "Is this your gun? Did you shoot that woman who ran out of here? "

I explained the situation and flopped down in one of the pews again. I couldn't move.

"This is a church, not a war zone," he said. "You'll have to leave. I don't want the police or that woman or anyone connected with all this in here. Leave."

He was tugging at my arm trying to make me get up and go. My legs wouldn't work.

"Just let me call someone to come and get me," I said, speaking as calmly as I could. "I don't mean to cause you any trouble. I just can't walk at the moment. My friends will take me out of here, and you'll never hear from me again. I promise."

It was the first time in my life a minister tried to get me to *leave* a church.

He stopped pulling at my arm. "Well, hurry. Please. I can't have this going on in my sanctuary." He handed me the gun. "And take this with you. It doesn't belong here."

I put the gun in my bag and pulled out my phone to call Tina.

"Weezie!" she said. "Where are you? How come you didn't show up for rehearsal this afternoon? We were worried about you. Peter's going to drive us home."

"I'm . . ." I realized I had no idea where I was. I looked questioningly at the minister. "Where am I, Reverend?"

"You're at Sixth Avenue and Thirty-Fifth Street," he said. "Tell them to hurry."

I told Tina where I was and what had happened. She said Peter would be there in a few minutes, and I should wait outside the church.

I held onto the pew in front of me and pulled myself to my feet. I didn't want to leave this safe place. Or at least I thought it was safe until Shelli turned up with a gun. Where was she? Maybe she was waiting for me outside the church.

"Could I just stay inside the church, by the front door, to wait for my friends?" I asked.

"I guess so," the minister said. "But I don't want any more trouble or gunshots in here."

I knew I should shut up but I couldn't help saying to him, "Aren't you supposed to help people in trouble? You know, like Jesus told us to do?"

"There weren't any guns in Jesus's day," he said. "Even he would want you out of this church."

He had a point. I opened the door of the church a crack so I could see Peter's car when he drove up. There was no sign of Shelli out front, but I had a terrible feeling that I hadn't seen the last of her.

I was never so glad to see anybody as I was to see Peter's handsome, worried face when his van pulled up to the church. I ran outside and jumped into the car and my friends gathered me up in a big hug. They could see how shaken I was. My purse fell open when I sat down and the gun fell on the floor.

"Be careful," I said. "It's loaded."

"Give it to me," Peter said. "You have to report guns in your possession to the police when you don't have a license to carry one. The last thing we need is for you to be arrested for owning a gun. You can give this gun to Detective Carver when you see him tomorrow."

"Weezie," Gini said, "for a housewife, you're leading far too exciting a life. Where'd you get the gun?"

"Didn't Tina tell you?" I said, a couple of minutes later when I could talk again.

"It was hard to understand you when you called," Tina said. "I heard something about Shelli and a gun and that you were in a church. None of it made much sense, Weez. All I knew was that we had to come and get you—fast."

"Thank God you did," I said. "She was going to kill me with that gun. I managed to knock it out of her hand and the minister came and she ran out of the church and now is I don't know where . . ." I put my face in my hands and started to cry. It all caught up with me. I'm just not cut out for this stuff.

Pat put her arms around me and held me while I cried. She rocked me back and forth.

"It's okay, sweetie," she said. "Let it all out. You have a right to cry."

Peter reached over the seat and touched my hair. "You'll be home soon, Mary Louise," he said. "You're safe."

He started the van and pulled away from the curb and headed toward the tunnel. My friends all murmured comforting things to me. Finally, I stopped crying and wiped my eyes.

"Sorry, guys," I said. "I don't mean to be such a wuss."

"You're not a wuss, hon," Tina said. "Your life was in danger."

"From now on, I'm staying home and cooking," I said. "The worst thing that can happen is a little bacon grease spattering on my hand when I make my trout wrapped in bacon."

"I love that dish," Gini said. "When are you going to make it again? Can I come? Okay if I bring Alex?"

Talk about food always cheers me up.

"I'm going to have a huge dinner party for all of us and our partners," I said. "I'll make the trout and all kinds of yummy things. From now on, I'm only dancing in my own living room."

"Riiiiiight," Peter said.

Mary Louise's Cooking Tip: If someone is pointing a gun at you, don't feel you have to offer them a snack.

Chapter 15

Could Somebody Please Get The Door?

When I got home, I looked in the fridge to see what to cook for George. Cooking was such a normal thing to do. Much better than having a gun stuck in my side. And Shelli was still out there. I turned the handle of the back door. It was unlocked. I turned the lock and put the chain up. This was ridiculous. I was afraid in my own house. Where was George? It was past time for him to be home after his weekly squash game with one of the guys in his firm. And come to think of it, where was Tucker? He usually bounded out to greet me whenever I walked in the house. He must be asleep somewhere, I decided.

I checked the fridge again. Some chopped beef. Some chicken breasts. Leftover swordfish and tomato sauce. That would be the easiest. I could make some spaghetti and heat up the sauce. A nice salad and we'd have a good dinner. I put the sauce out on the counter and stuck a large pot of water on the stove to bring to a boil for the spaghetti.

I went back into the living room to read the paper until George got home. Where was he anyway? It was past seven. He was usually home by this time. I clicked his number on my phone. A few rings and then his voicemail. He must be driving home and couldn't answer his phone. Yes, that was it. He'd be walking in that door any minute.

I went back in the kitchen to make the salad dressing. I listened to the news on CNN while I worked. Mostly news about the election coming up. I only listened with half an ear because I'd heard all this before.

The front door opened. Oh, thank God. George was home. I ran into the living room and clung to him before he could take off his coat.

"I'm so glad you're home," I said. "You're late. What happened to you?"

He kissed me and held me close. "You know, honey, you're getting to be a nervous wreck with this job."

I burrowed into his chest. "I know, I know," I said. "But you have no idea what happened to me today, George. I don't know how I'm still alive."

He took off his coat and led me gently to the couch.

"What happened?" he said.

When I told him about Marlowe threatening my life again, about Shelli in the church with a gun, about Shelli out there somewhere, he took my face in his hands and made himself speak calmly.

"You can't go on like this, Mary Louise," he said. "How come you didn't call me? I can't believe you went through all that and didn't call me."

I realized I had to tell him.

"George, Mike came to get me. I called Mike."

"You called Mike instead of me?"

"He's in the city, George. I needed someone right away. He saved me from Marlowe."

His face changed. "I was in the city working on that case with the elevator shaft. You must have known that. You could have called my cell. Why didn't you call me?"

"It's Saturday," I said. "I didn't know you were going into the city today. I just didn't think, George. I was so scared."

He asked me the question that was torturing him.

"Are you in love with him?" he said. "Tell me the truth. Are you?"

"I thought I was," I said. He winced. "But I know now that I really love you and I told him that today. He asked me if we could still be friends, and I said I'd find out how you felt about that."

"I wish you wouldn't see him anymore," he said. "That's how I feel. I'd worry all the time that you'd decide you loved him instead of me. If you loved him once, you could love him again." His voice broke. "I just don't want to lose you."

"Then I won't see him anymore," I said.

"Thank you," he said. "But tell me how he saved your life today."

I told him the whole story about Marlowe hiding in the ladies' room at the Music Hall and taking me out of there at gunpoint. How she told me she was going to take me to Cuba, and Mike got there in time to rescue me, and then about the church and Shelli and the gun.

"What are you in—some kind of horror movie?" he said. "You went through all that and then came home and fixed dinner?"

I started to laugh. It wasn't really funny, but when he put it like that, it did seem unreal. Somebody held a gun against my side twice in one day, and I still came home to make dinner. Why wasn't I huddled in a corner in a mental institution somewhere?

"I keep thinking Shelli is going to turn up again," I said. "I know it's crazy but every time I hear the door open I think it's her. Even when you came in just now."

"She doesn't even know where you live. Why don't you quit this job, Mary Louise?" he said. "It's not worth it."

"We were going to quit, but as I told you this

morning, Tina asked us to help out Bianca, the new head of the Rockettes because she was really stuck with five of her best dancers gone. I thought I was safe."

"You've got to get Carver to assign a policeman to stay with you until they get Shelli. Please call him now."

I realized he was right. I couldn't fool around with this anymore. I picked up the phone and called Detective Carver. I told him what had happened in the church with Shelli and that she had escaped. "It's getting so I'm afraid to go out of the house," I said to him. "George wanted me to call you to ask if I could have police protection."

"Of course," he said. "I'll have somebody report to you right away."

I thanked him and hung up. I told George what he said and he looked relieved.

"Thank God," he said. "I worry about you all the time. Is the police officer coming here to the house?"

"I think so," I said. "He didn't really say, but that's what I assume."

I went out to the kitchen to make the spaghetti with swordfish sauce. The water came to a boil and I had just plunked the pasta into the pot when there was a knock at the back door. I was relieved that Detective Carver had managed to get a policeman to our house that fast. I was constantly impressed with what that detective could achieve.

I pulled back the chain, unlocked the door and opened it wide.

"Don't make a sound," Shelli said. She was holding a gun. "Be very quiet, and you and your husband won't get hurt. I need you to get me out of this country."

"I thought you were going to take that boat to Cuba with Marlowe," I said, speaking loudly so George would hear me.

"Very funny," she said. "You knew Marlowe had been arrested and that there was no longer any boat waiting for her when you told me that lie in the church. I went there after I left you, and of course there was no boat and no Marlowe. I googled you and found out where you lived. You're going to get me out of here."

"How do you think I'm going to—"

The kitchen door swung open and George said, "Who are you?"

He saw Shelli standing there with a gun. "Oh my God!"

"Don't move," she said, "or I'll shoot her. I've got to get out of here. You're going to drive me to a place on the Jersey Shore where a friend of mine has a boat. He wants to get out of this country too. I'll be holding a gun on your cute little wife here until I get on that boat. Understand?"

I understand," George said. "We'll do whatever you say. Do you want to leave now?"

"I need something to eat first. Anything. I haven't eaten all day and I feel weak. You"—she pointed her gun at me—"give me something. Anything. And then we'll go. It's better to drive there at night."

"The spaghetti should be ready," I said, putting

on my potholder mitts to lift up the pot of boiling water full of cooked spaghetti. I started toward the sink to pour the spaghetti into the colander, but turned suddenly and threw the contents of the pot into Shelli's face. She screamed, dropped the gun, and covered her face with her hands.

George grabbed the gun from the floor and pointed it at Shelli who ran to the sink and splashed cold water on her face. The back door flew open and a police officer ran in, his gun out.

"What's happening?" he said, looking from George holding a gun, to Shelli crying and holding her face under the faucet, to me with an empty pot, and spaghetti all over the kitchen floor.

The officer assumed that George was the bad guy and Shelli was the innocent victim crying and bent over the sink. I don't know what he thought I was doing standing there in the middle of a pile of thin spaghetti.

"Drop that gun," the officer said to George, who immediately did so. The officer took out handcuffs and was going to put them on George when I yelled, "No, No, officer, he's my husband. I'm Mary Louise Temple. Detective Carver called you to protect me. That woman came here to get us to drive her to the Jersey shore and—"

The officer looked totally confused. "What was your husband doing with a gun? What's wrong with her?"

"Call Detective Carver," I said. "He'll explain the whole thing to you."

Shelli wiped the water out of her eyes and tried to get to the back door, but I wasn't going to let her get away twice in one day. I took the heavy pot and hit her on the back of the head. She fell to the floor.

The police officer took out his phone and clicked on a number.

"Sir," he said. "This is Officer Santiago. I'm at the home of Mr. and Mrs. Temple as you asked. But there seems to be some . . ." He listened for a minute and then said, "Well, sir, there's a young woman here and I don't know who . . ." His face changed as he listened to the detective on the other end, who must have explained the whole situation to him. "I'll arrest her immediately, sir."

He clicked off the phone and leaned down to put handcuffs on Shelli when she brought her foot up and kicked him in the groin. He groaned. She was almost up and out the door when George tripped her and slammed the door shut. She fell down again and the police officer handcuffed her.

George and the police officer pulled Shelli out to the car, the officer's gun against her back.

As she was being put into the car, Shelli said to me, "You haven't seen the last of me."

"You've seen the last of her and everybody else for a long time," the officer said as he closed the police car door. I slammed the back door behind them and collapsed into a kitchen chair, shaking and crying. How did I ever get mixed up with murderers and crazy people? I was this nice person, raised by good parents, married to a fine man—a lawyer for heavens' sake—the mother of three excellent children, a tap dancer! In the last two days, I had had a loaded gun pointed at me four times. How could this happen?

I jumped when the kitchen door swung open. It was George with Tucker right behind him, wagging his tail and coming over to bump against my leg.

"You're some watchdog," I said, hugging him and holding on to him tightly. I held his face in my hands. "Where were you when I needed you?"

He nuzzled me again, his tail sweeping back and forth so rapidly I thought he'd knock a chair over.

George and I looked at the spaghetti all over the floor, a wet mess.

"What do you want on your spaghetti, George?" I said, and we collapsed into each other's arms, laughing helplessly.

RECIPE FOR SPAGHETTI WITH SWORDFISH IN TOMATO SAUCE

Serves 4

2 lb. swordfish cut up in one-inch cubes
¼ cup olive oil
2 garlic cloves, minced
1 cup parsley, chopped
2 tsp. fennel seed
¼ tsp. hot red pepper flakes
1 35-oz. can crushed plum tomatoes
½ tsp. salt
1 lb. spaghetti

1. Preheat oven to 400 degrees.
2. Heat water for the spaghetti in a six-quart pot.
3. Put the oil in a saucepan and cook the garlic until it sizzles.
4. Add parsley, fennel seed, and hot red pepper, and cook for about 4 minutes, stirring constantly.
5. Add tomatoes and salt and simmer for about five minutes.
6. Spread the swordfish cubes out in a 9 x 13-inch baking dish.
7. Pour the tomato sauce over the swordfish and cook in the oven for 20 minutes.
8. Cook the spaghetti during the last 10 minutes the swordfish is in the oven.
9. Drain the spaghetti and pour the delicious sauce over it for a fantastically good meal.

Mary Louise's cooking tip: If your idea of a great meal is a nice mixed-green salad, don't invite anybody over for dinner.

Chapter 16

Merry Christmas!

We didn't exactly become the Rockettes, but we worked hard over the next few weeks to get as close to them as we could. Bianca assigned us to some seasoned dancers who worked us every day until we swung into our Santa routines with practiced, precise swings and turns and kicks. After we achieved this agility, it even became fun to practice every day. We even managed to smile as we got better.

Bianca was true to her word and had special costumes made for us that were light and brief, showing off our legs and our new slimmer figures. They were red Santa jackets without the forty-pound weights in them and with adorable little white furry buttons down the front. We wore Santa hats with fluffy white balls on top that bounced when we moved.

The choreographer invented a dance for us that was fast and funny and a nice contrast to the rest of the show.

On opening night in November, we got a nice round of applause when we finished our part, and most nights for the rest of the run we were a hit. We danced with the rest of the cast through the Christmas holidays, and I threw a big dinner party for my friends after we finished.

Mary Louise's Cooking Tip: If you make cheese puffs for your guests, try not to eat half of them before the guests arrive.

Chapter 17

Come For Dinner

I love giving dinner parties. And this one was going to be spectacular. I wanted to make all my favorite dishes for my Hoofer friends who would soon be scattered all over the world. Who knew when we would all be together again? I was determined to make this last night one they would always remember.

Early in the day I put extra leaves in the dining room table so it would be long enough for ten people. I spread my best white linen tablecloth on it. I wanted a plain but elegant background for my great-grandmother's Crown Ducal china, which was unlike any other dinnerware I had ever seen.

To begin with, it wasn't round; it was octagonal. It had flowers blooming all over it. Not just along the edges or in the middle but winding all over the plates. Red roses, yellow daffodils, pale blue morning glories, dark blue violets, green and brown vines graced the white background. It was like eating in a garden.

My great-grandmother was a crotchety old lady, according to most accounts, but she certainly knew how to choose china. When she died, these Crown Ducals went to my grandmother, who cherished them and then passed them along to my mother, who gave them to me when she no longer hosted elaborate dinner parties.

My great-grandmother and great-grandfather were of Scottish descent. Their families moved to Canada, where my great-grandparents met and married, then emigrated to Boston. There in that musty old city, my great-grandfather worked for a carriage company in the last part of the nineteenth century and the first part of the twentieth. That was fine until some thoughtless person invented the automobile, and carriages were way out of date.

But during the years that people still needed carriages to attach to their horses, my great-grandparents and their son, my grandfather, managed to scrounge out a life in Boston. My grandfather used to walk across the bridge to MIT every day while he earned an electrical engineering degree, which led to his lifetime job at Bell Laboratories.

I think Scottish ancestry and hard work are synonymous. My parents taught me the value of hard work, honesty, and love. So my great-grandmother's china was not only beautiful but a reminder of those hardworking Scots who brought up my grandfather, who raised my father, who taught me to treasure the good life I was blessed to lead and the lovely things that surrounded me every day.

It gave me such pleasure to put those plates around the table at each of the places where my closest friends and their loves would be dining that evening. I took my silver out of its tarnish-proof cloth and put the knives and forks and spoons carefully at each place setting. Then I set wine glasses above each knife that would be filled with a deliciously dry Sauvignon blanc. Matching butter plates went above the forks, and I was finished.

Next came the flowers I had bought that morning. In addition to the crystal vase of dark red roses in the middle of the table, I put little white Limoges pitchers, each holding a single pink rose, at each plate.

When I finished, I stepped back and reveled in the sight of that lovely table, full of centuries-old china that would delight twenty-first-century women and their partners.

Now all I had to do was prepare the food to put on those plates. I was going to fix my favorite dinner for my favorite people in the world. It took a while to make, but it was worth the trouble: my incredibly delicious trout, which I stuffed with onions, then wrapped in bacon and cooked in the oven and served with a rosemary cream sauce. I could get the whole thing ready ahead of time and then bake it at the last minute.

I'd serve rice and a salad with it. I had already made my vinaigrette dressing so it would mellow before I put it on the salad and French bread to go with the whole deal. And for dessert I would make my famous frozen lemon souffle, covered with raspberries, that I learned how to make in Paris when we danced on the *Bateau Mouche*.

I went into the living room, which would be softly lit, graced with bouquets of flowers on the end tables and coffee table, ready for these people who had brought so much joy into my life.

Back to the kitchen to start my trout and stir up some cheese puffs to go with our drinks before dinner. These little puffs were simple but perfect. I opened a jar of sharp cheddar Cheese, which I had left out to soften, and mixed it with half a stick of butter, also softened. Next, I threw in a half a cup of sifted flour and half a teaspoon of salt and smooshed it all together until it was thoroughly mixed. Then I made little round balls of the mixture, flattened them out, and put them on a greased cookie sheet, ready to go into a 350-degree oven for fifteen minutes. They came out crispy little cheese puffs that nobody could resist.

A friendly bump against my leg reminded me I had better put them out of Tucker's reach.

"They're not for you, old dog," I said, leaning over to give him a hug. "You get your usual food." He wagged his tail furiously while I dumped some dog food into his dish.

"How about me?" George said, coming into the kitchen and giving me a hug. "Do I get some of those or dog food?"

"I'll think about it," I said, giving him a kiss.

"What can I do to help?" he asked.

"Mostly stay out of my way," I said. "I'll be puttering and cooking all day. You can make sure the wine is chilled and get the liquor out of the cabinet for drinks if you want. That would be great."

"What are you making?"

"My bacon-wrapped trout and my frozen lemon souffle for dessert."

"Do these people know how lucky they are?" he said.

"I feel sad that we're all separating and won't be together for a while after we finish the Christmas show," I said. "I want to send them off in style."

"Tell me again where everyone is going so I can keep it straight tonight," George said.

"Let's see," I said, leaning against the counter and sorting everybody out in my mind. "Alex and Gini are going to India to get their little girl, and—"

"Were they actually able to arrange that with the Indian government? I thought it was practically impossible."

"It was very difficult, but somehow Alex used

his connections with The *Times* to get the adoption approved."

"Are they going to get married when they get back?"

"Oh, you know Gini," I said. "She doesn't see any reason to get married. She says they're perfectly happy the way they are. Maybe she's right."

"Legally, she'd be better off married," George said. "But nobody can tell Gini what to do or not do, legally or not."

"You're right there," I said. "And of course you know Peter and Tina are getting married in January at the Frick."

"Finally," George said. "Took them long enough."

"It took Tina long enough," I said. "Peter has been ready for a long time."

"What about Janice and Tom?" he asked. "Aren't they getting married on that old boat in Brooklyn?"

"Yes," I said. "But don't call it that. It's the Bargemusic and it's lovely. Just right for Tom and Janice."

"When is that?" George asked.

"They haven't decided. They're going on a honeymoon in San Sebastian in Spain first. We almost got there when we danced on that train in northern Spain, but a couple of murders got in the way—remember?"

"I remember," he said. He looked serious. We were both remembering that I met Mike on that train.

"And Pat and Denise are taking David to Disneyland," I said to change the subject. "He's never been and neither have they."

"So you're the only one left at home," George said. "I'm glad. I'll have you all to myself. You don't have any jobs coming up in Afghanistan, do you?"

I laughed. "No job in Afghanistan, Iraq, or Iran," I said. "I'll just hang out here and dance for you."

He held me close. "I almost lost you," he said. "I'll never let that happen again. I love you, Mary Louise."

"I love you," I said. And this time I really meant it. I pulled away from him. "Now get out of here and let me make my trout."

He grabbed Tucker's leash from the hook on the wall and called to him. "Come on Tucker. Let's get out of the way before she wraps us in bacon too."

Tucker bounded over to let George attach the leash, and they left for a walk.

Mary Louise's Cooking tip: It's not enough to cook with love. You need some good recipes!

Chapter 18

New York, New York!

That night my house was its most beautiful self. My friends were coming at six and we would eat and talk the night away, grateful to be together and alive.

George came downstairs looking handsome in a blazer and slacks. He checked the bar to make sure he hadn't forgotten anything. There was a bottle of really old Scotch, some dry vermouth and vodka for martinis, sweet vermouth and rye for my manhattan, Sauvignon blanc for the white-wine drinkers chilling in an ice bucket, and a Cabernet and a Pinot noir for the red winers. And, of course, some lemonade for Pat and Denise.

George turned away from the bar and whistled when he looked at me.

"You're beautiful," he said.

I was wearing a silky blue dress, cut low in the front and pleated all around in the skirt. It was George's favorite dress. I always felt fantastic when I wore it.

He put his arms around me and held me close to him.

"You smell good," he said.

"Must be the bacon spattered in my hair," I said.

He laughed. "Must be," he said. "Or maybe it's the trout on your chin."

The doorbell rang and we went to greet the first of our arrivals, Gini and Alex. Gini looked stunning in a black-and-white top and pants, and Alex actually had on a tie and was wearing a suit.

"Come in, come in," I said. "You're the first."

"Good," Gini said. "I can drink one of your incredible martinis undisturbed, George."

"Got any Scotch, George?" Alex asked.

"That's like asking Donald Trump if he has any money," Gini said.

We were laughing when Tina, accompanied by Peter, opened the front door. "What's so funny?" she asked."

"Just another Donald Trump joke," Gini said, giving her and Peter a hug.

George took their coats and went to get the wine they asked for, when the bell rang again and Pat and Denise came in to join us.

"Lemonade, you two?" George asked.

"For Pat," Denise said, "but I think I'll have one of your martinis, George. I hear they're phenomenal."

"They are, actually," George said and went to make her a practically vermouthless martini.

"We're all here except Janice and Tom," I said. "Sit down everybody, and I'll bring you my cheese puffs."

"Janice is always late," Gini said. "I don't think she can tell time."

"I heard that," Janice said, opening the door and pulling Tom into the room with her. "Haven't you ever heard the saying 'Save the best till last?' "

"Right," I said hugging her and taking her coat. She looked superb as always in a red dress with silver buttons. "You are the best, Jan. What are you drinking?"

"Think I'll have a glass of Champagne."

"Too bad," George said. "That's the only thing I don't have. Will you settle for a Sauvignon blanc?"

"When the lady asks for Champagne," Tom said, "the lady gets Champagne." And he thrust a chilled bottle of Dom Pérignon into George's hands. "This is to celebrate us all being alive," he said.

If I had been Catholic, I would have crossed myself at that point. I might not have been there to drink that Champagne if Marlowe or Shelli had been successful in their attempts to kill me several days in a row.

Usually I would have had a manhattan because George made the best ones, but a glass of Champagne seemed just right for tonight. I went out to the kitchen and took my cheese puffs out of the oven and brought them into the living room.

"Attention, *mes amis*," I said, raising my glass of Champagne. "Here's to the Happy Hoofers and the people we love. May we dance until we're a hundred and two!"

Cheers and *Here's to us!* rang out. Tucker banged his tail on the floor to express his delight at being part of this celebration.

"Before we settle down to serious eating," Tina said, "could you guys give me some travel trips for my article on New York? I'm so used to going in and out of the city, I can't think like a tourist about it. What should we tell our honeymooners coming to New York for the first time?"

"Bring a large basket of money," Gini said.

"Come on now," Tina said. "There are lots of free things you can do in New York. Help me think of them."

"All of Central Park is free," I said. "You can walk around or sit by a pond near the Alice in Wonderland statue or go see the Imagine memorial to John Lennon."

"That's good," Tina said. "But they'll probably discover that by themselves. I want to tell them about some free things they wouldn't know about if we didn't tell them."

"I made a list once," Gini said, "of times when you can get into the museums—which are usually really expensive—for free. It's because I'm cheap. The ones I remember are the American

Museum of Natural History, which is free the last hour every day, from four forty-five to five forty-five. At other times, the admission price is just suggested, so if you have the nerve to do it, you can just not take their suggestion and walk in free."

"I always feel too guilty to do that," Pat said.

"You feel guilty if you don't wash your hands every time you sneeze," Denise said.

"Well, I can't help it," Pat said. "I'd rather go to a museum when I know it's free. Like the Museum of Modern Art is free from four to eight in the afternoon on Fridays. So that's when I go. And I don't have to feel guilty."

"I'll still love you even if you sneak into the Natural History Museum without paying," Denise said.

The two friends smiled at each other. I loved seeing those two together.

"That was a good one," Tina said. "What else?"

"The Neue Galerie is free from six to eight on the first Friday of the month," Alex said. "The *Times* did a whole article on free times in museums. I'll email it to you, Tina."

"Thanks, Alex," Tina said, making a note on her iPad.

"You can pay whatever you wish, including nothing, at the New York Aquarium at three o'clock on Fridays during the year, and four in the summer," Peter said.

"I love boats," Janice said. "Especially yours, Peter. When you're not around, I jump on the Staten Island Ferry or the ferry to Governor's

Island in the summer when it's hot. They're both free. Sometimes I don't even get off the boat. I just ride it there and back. Lovely."

"Did you ever go to the Downtown Boathouse, where they have free kayaks to take out?" Peter asked. "It's really fun, Jan. You'd love it."

"I think I want somebody else to drive the boat," Janice said. "You have to come with me, Peter!"

I went out to the kitchen and got my platter of little pastry shells filled with a mixture of cream cheese, sour cream, onion, and red caviar. They were bite-size and favorites of my friends.

I passed the shells and napkins around to everybody.

"These are the best things I've ever eaten," Peter said. "Are they free?"

"No, they'll cost you a kiss," I said, leaning over so he could plant a kiss on my cheek.

"Leave my fiancé alone and think up something else free in New York," Tina said.

"How about the High Line?" Denise said. "That's always fun to do and totally free."

"Perfect," Tina said. "Where does it go—from what street to what street?"

"From Gansevoort to Thirtieth Street, between Ninth and Eleventh Avenues," she said. "And it's always different. Flowers and shrubs. Shops and people watching. You go along a wooden walk above the city where train tracks used to be and get a great view of what goes on below you. As well as beside you."

"There's the Bronx Zoo too," Pat added. "It's free on Wednesdays. Or I should say, you can pay what you want, and it's the one place I allow myself to not pay."

"Tsk, tsk," Gini said. "The Lord will get you for that, Pat."

"You forgot my favorite free thing in New York," George said. "That pianist who plays classical music in Washington Square. He brings his own piano and plays there when the weather is nice."

"He's wonderful," I said. "People donate money to a box on the piano, but you can just sit there all day and listen for nothing if you want."

"These are all excellent," Tina said. "But I should put in some warnings about things not to do in New York. Any suggestions?"

"There are a lot of places you should avoid on weekends because they're too crowded," Alex said. "It's not fun to go on the High Line, for instance, on a weekend because it's full of New Yorkers as well as tourists. Same for Times Square and the top of the Empire State Building. Or the Metropolitan Museum or the Museum of Modern Art, which are packed on weekends. "

"And don't go on the subways during rush hour, either," Gini said. "You can't move. You get squashed."

"But you should tell them to take the subways other times," Pat said. "People tend to take taxis everywhere when they come to the city and that's really expensive. And if you're in a hurry, taxis get stuck in traffic jams. Tell them to get a subway map and get around that way."

"Good idea," Tina said. "What else shouldn't they do?"

"I always feel sorry for those people on tour buses," Denise said. "They just get glimpses of the city. It's better to find a walking tour or get a city map and explore the city on your own."

"Not everybody can do that, though, Denise," Tina said. "If you've never been to New York before, it can be confusing."

"You can usually get street maps in the hotel where you're staying," I said. "And tell your honeymooners they shouldn't be afraid to ask directions from New Yorkers hurrying by them. They may look unfriendly, but if you stop someone and ask for help, most people will be glad to give you directions and a few kind words."

"I love New Yorkers," Janice said. "They always help me whenever I need it."

"It's because you're so ugly they feel sorry for you," Gini said.

"Thank you, Gini, dear," Janice said, sprinkling some pastry crumbs into Gini's drink.

"A few more helpful hints and then dinner will be ready," I said.

"I've got one," George said. "Tell them not to eat only in chain restaurants that they can go to in their own home towns. Tell them to ask someone in the hotel for the names of some inexpensive, good restaurants in the city and eat there."

"I like that one, George," Tina said. "In fact, I think I'll include a list of some affordable places at the end of the article. I think I've got enough now, gang. Thanks for all this."

"Oh wait, Tina, I have one more," Janice said. "Tell them not to wear flipflops when they walk around New York. I know they're used to wearing them at home in the summertime, but in New York their feet will be grimy by the time they get back to their hotel at the end of the day. And if someone steps on their toes, they'll be sorry."

"Uh, speaking of honeymooners," Tina said and shot a questioning look at Peter.

"Oh go ahead, tell them," he said. "You know you're bursting to."

"Well," Tina said looking around the room at all of us.

"Spit it out, for heaven's sake," Gini said in her usual tactful way.

"Okay, here goes," Tina said, taking a deep breath. "We've been offered a great job in January."

"Where?" Gini said. "What do you mean January? You're getting married in January and I'm going to India and Janice is going to Spain and Pat's going to Disneyland. Mary Louise is the only one who's available."

"I promised George I—" I started to say.

"Cool it, Gini," Tina said. "I haven't signed us up for anything yet. It's just that this nightclub in London in the West End—you know, near all the theaters—asked us to come and dance for a week during their slow time in January. They heard about our dancing on the *Bateau Mouche* in Paris and wondered if we were available. I said I'd see."

"Now wait a minute, Tina," Pat said. "Won't

you be on your honeymoon in January? You've got your whole wedding planned at the Frick, and then I thought you and Peter were going to St. Bart's. Where it's warm."

"Well, we did sort of plan on St. Bart's," Tina said. "But then this man with a great British accent called and asked me if we were free. Peter said London was fine with him for a honeymoon. But if you all have other plans, I'll just tell him it's impossible."

"Are you nuts, Peter?" Gini said in her most exasperated tone. "You'd rather go to London in January in the rain and fog and cold for your honeymoon than lie in the sun in St. Bart's?"

"I learned long ago that anywhere I go with Tina is just fine," Peter said, smiling at his bride-to-be. "Knowing her, she'll make cold, rainy London as wonderful as hot old St. Bart's."

We looked at these two people who were obviously destined to have a long and happy life together. Nobody said anything for a while.

Then Pat spoke up. "Well, Denise and I can certainly take David to Disneyland in February," she said. "It won't make that much difference to him. David is very adaptable.

Denise nodded in agreement. "Of course," she said.

"George loves London," I said. "Don't you, honey?"

"I do," he said. "I should be able to arrange it. Depends on when this trial is scheduled." He put his arm around me and gave me a hug.

Alex looked at Gini. "We can go to India from London," he said. "It's only another week."

"I suppose," she said, not looking pleased, but then she never does at first. We all knew she would come around.

"What about your trip to San Sebastian, Janice?" Tina asked her. "I thought you had it all planned as sort of a pre-wedding honeymoon. Are you okay about going to London instead?"

Janice looked at Tom.

"We can go to Spain right after London," he said. "It's closer than going there from New York. What do you think, Jan?"

Janice smiled. "That's fine," she said. "I love London. Even in January."

"Then we're all agreed we'll go to London after we finish in New York and after our wedding?" Tina said

We all raised our glasses and cheered.

"To London," Alex said.

"Á la table, everyone," I said, and my friends and I all joined each other at my table for dinner, excited about a chance to dance again.

Are you in a London mood? We'd love to have you join us.

RECIPE FOR TROUT AND BACON

Serves 6

¾ cup balsamic vinegar
1½ cups water
2 large onions, sliced
⅓ cup sugar
4 tsp. fresh rosemary leaves, chopped
2 cups chicken broth
1 cup heavy cream
6 trout, skin on the bottom, heads and tails
    removed
24 slices bacon (you might need more,
    depending on how thick the bacon is)
1 T. olive oil

Preheat oven to 450 degrees.
1. Boil first five ingredients in a saucepan for about seven minutes. Just make sure the onions are cooked.
2. Drain the onion mixture but save the liquid it cooked in and reduce it to ¾ cup.
3. Add the chicken broth and boil it until you have about 1½ cups left. You can prepare the trout while this is boiling.
4. Spread the trout out and fill each one with the onion mixture.
5. Fold up the trout around the onion and wrap bacon slices around each trout so that they overlap, completely encircling the fish. You might need more than four slices of bacon for each fish.
6. Brown the trout in the olive oil until the bacon is cooked.

7. While the trout and bacon are cooking and the bacon is nicely browning, add the cup of heavy cream to the broth that is boiling on the stove and let it simmer until it's reduced to 2 cups. Reach over and stir it every once in a while when you're not tending to the trout.

8. When your bacon is beautifully brown, transfer the trout to an oiled pan and bake it in the oven for 20 minutes.

9. When the creamy broth is reduced to its proper amount, pour it into the pan the trout browned in and stir it all up to get the flavorful brown bits in the bottom of the pan.

10. Pour the sauce over the trout and serve. Be prepared for a lot of compliments.

RECIPE FOR VINAIGRETTE
SALAD DRESSING

Makes one cup

4 tsp. Dijon mustard
Salt and pepper to taste
1 tsp. minced garlic
8 tsp. red wine vinegar
1 cup vegetable oil
1 tsp. dried rosemary

1. Mix the garlic, vinegar, salt, and pepper together thoroughly in a bowl.
2. Whisk in the oil, but do it very gradually, until the dressing is the right thickness. You don't want it to be watery. You might not need the whole cup of oil.

RECIPE FOR CHEESE PUFFS

Makes about 24 puffs

1 jar Kraft Old English Sharp Cheddar Cheese
   or similar product, softened
½ stick salted butter, also softened.
½ cup sifted flour
½ tsp. salt

1. Moosh all ingredients together and roll them
up into little balls.
2. Flatten the balls and place them on a greased
cookie sheet.
3. Bake at 350 degrees for 15 minutes.

The precise number of balls each recipe makes
depends on how small or large you make the
balls.

RECIPE FOR PASTRY SHELLS
WITH CAVIAR

Makes 32 shells

Dough:
½ cup water
¼ tsp. salt
Dash cayenne
4 T. butter
½ cup flour
2 eggs

Filling:
4 T. cream cheese, softened
½ cup sour cream
½ cup red or black caviar
1 T. grated onion

Preheat oven to 375 degrees
1. Bring water, salt, cayenne and butter to a boil in a saucepan.
2. Add flour and stir over low heat until it turns into a ball of dough.
3. Take the pan off the heat and add the eggs to the dough, beating them until the dough is nice and glossy.
4. Grease a flat baking pan with butter.
5. Put 32 teaspoons of the dough on the baking pan. Leave space between them for the cooked shells to spread out.
6. Bake about 20 minutes until they are brown. Let them cool while you make the filling.

7. Blend the cream cheese and the sour cream.
8. Carefully add the caviar and onion so the caviar doesn't mush up.
9. Split the shells and fill them with the divine caviar mixture, and try to be modest when everyone raves about them at your party.

Acknowledgments

I want to thank New York for all the adventures I've had there: for the interesting friends I've made in the city, especially Michaela Hamilton, my editor at Kensington; for the chance to ride on the merry-go-rounds in Bryant Park and Brooklyn Heights; for the plays I've seen; for the museums I've loved; for the people I see in this city I'd never see anywhere else.

Did you miss the first book in the Happy Hoofers Mystery Series? Turn the page to read the delightful opening chapters from *Chorus Lines, Caviar, and Corpses*!

Available from Kensington Publishing Corp.

Chapter 1

Keeping On Our Toes

It all started when Mary Louise decided we needed to exercise. We are five close friends, who've all managed to stay fit over the years. Still, when we moved into our fifties, we knew we had to watch what we ate and become more active.

We considered all the ways there are to exercise. What we really loved was dancing, especially tap dancing, so we took a class and worked out some routines. Before long, we were asked to perform at a local senior center . . . and then at a community service luncheon . . . and one gig led to another. Pretty soon the word was out about the fabulous five fifty-somethings with the high kicks, smooth moves, and bright smiles. Our video on YouTube got hundreds of hits.

Who knew we'd get to be so good that someone would hire us to dance on the *Smirnov*, a
Russian ship sailing up the Volga from Moscow
to St. Petersburg? That we would encounter a
stern German cruise director named Heidi, a
disgruntled British chef who loved to drink but
wasn't fond of cooking, and a motley crew that
never did master the art of graceful service?

We thought we would eat some good food, meet
some nice people, see things we'd never seen before, and get paid for it. What could go wrong?

Plenty, as it turned out. If I'd known ahead of
time that we'd get mixed up in a couple of murders and that my own life would be endangered
on this so-called pleasure trip, I would have
stayed happily at home in Champlain, New Jersey, commuting to New York to my job as a
travel editor at *Perfect Bride* magazine.

Let me tell you a bit about us.

Just briefly, there's me, Tina Powell, who for
better or worse is the leader of our little group
because I'm the most organized. Like our whole
gang, I'm in good shape because of our dancing. I weigh 110 pounds and am 5'4" tall. I don't
mention that I'm over fifty to strangers because
I can read their minds: *Drives a gas-guzzling SUV.
Wrapped up in her kids. Belongs to a book club that
reads Jane Austen and never gets around to discussing
the book. Botox."* I loved telling my coworkers at
Perfect Bride magazine, where I'm the travel editor, that my friends and I were hired to dance on
a cruise ship in Russia. Their usual reaction was,
"You mean they're actually going to pay you?" I

would just nod and smile. Besides dancing on this trip, I'm also writing an article for newly-weds who might want to honeymoon on this cruise.

Janice Rogers is an actress and director of shows in community theaters in our town. Since her divorce, she's been busier than ever, especially after her daughter went off to college. She's tall and blond and has an unlined face that never seems to age. Her skin has a glow that makes her look far younger than she is. When we ask her how she keeps her complexion like that, she says, "Neglect. I only wash it once a day. Soap is bad for your skin." She is a fierce friend, always there when you need her. I met her when she moved next door to me just after she and her husband split up.

Janice has long legs and, in black tights, they are stunning. "The legs are the last to go," she says. Actually, we all have great legs—it's just genetic, nothing we did or didn't do. And black stockings hide a multitude of sins.

Pat Keeler, a family therapist, our mother hen, watches over us. She's on the phone whenever she thinks it's necessary to make sure we're all right. She always remembers the tap routines. If we forget, we just look at Pat and do whatever she's doing. She is our rock. Her face is beautiful, with a few worry lines on her forehead. She's usually very serious, but when she smiles, it warms all of us. She's taller than the rest of us. Oh, and she's gay. It's just a fact of life with her. She doesn't flaunt it or hide it. Many of her clients are gay; she understands what they're going through. The rest of us are straight. Pat helps us with our problems too.

Mary Louise Temple has been my closest friend for over thirty years. We met when we both worked at *Redbook* magazine and became best friends. She has one of those Irish faces, with porcelain skin, dark hair, and blue, blue eyes. She somehow managed to keep a great body after three children and she thinks if you're not Irish, you should at least try. She's the only one who still has a husband, George, who believes it's his job to correct all the mistakes her parents made when they were bringing her up. I never could find any mistakes.

Finally, there's Gini Miller, a fierce redhead with a temper to match. She's a prize-winning documentary filmmaker, small and pretty. She's divorced. "We just wanted different things," she says of her ex-husband. "He was happy sitting on a couch with a beer watching football." She wanted to see the world. She filmed an oral history of the people who lost their homes in Hurricane Katrina in New Orleans. She made a documentary about an orphanage in India, where she fell in love with a little girl she hopes to adopt when regulations ease in that country.

We call ourselves the Happy Hoofers—that's with an *f*.

I love these women. The easy intimacy that the five of us enjoy has certainly helped to prepare us for life after fifty. We've been through everything together—miscarriages, sick children, husbands' affairs, cancer, widowhood, teenagers, divorce.

None of us could have done it without the other four cheering us on, lending a shoulder to cry on, saying just the right words to make everything better.

We are all different, all great-looking, and fierce friends forever.

Tina's Travel Tip: Talk to as many people as you can on a cruise—some of them might actually be interesting.

Chapter 2

Cruising and Schmoozing

I knew this wasn't going to be one of your Love Boat cruises the minute I opened the door to our cabin.

"Mary Louise, look at the size of this room! How can we change into our costumes in here?"

"Wait until you see the bathroom," she said. "There's no bath and I'd hardly call it a room. If we hadn't dieted ourselves into near nonexistence, we wouldn't be able to wash during the whole trip."

I looked over her shoulder and groaned. There was a basin, a toilet, and enough floor space for a very small three-year-old to take a shower.

"Where's the shower?" Mary Louise asked.

"I think you take the faucet off the basin and hang it on that hook up there, pull this curtain around you, and very carefully take a shower without breaking any of your movable parts."

"This is ridiculous," she said. "There's only two feet of floor space between the beds to change our clothes in. We'll have to dress in shifts."

"Too bad—I forgot to pack mine," I said, and we fell on the narrow beds laughing hysterically.

"Remind me again why we decided to take a Russian river cruise," she said.

"Because somebody actually hired us to tap dance on a ship sailing from Moscow to St. Petersburg," I said.

"What were they thinking!" she said.

"What were *we* thinking?" I said, and that set us off again. We couldn't help giggling at the absurdity of this whole situation. We've been friends for such a long time, we can read each other's thoughts. Ever since we met at *Redbook* magazine, where we both worked as editors before we were married, we've been good friends.

We've helped each other through babies— three for her and two for me—marital fights, and musicals at the community theater where she and I danced and sang our way to local stardom and total disdain from our teenagers. And the death of my husband a year ago. I could never have made it without her.

Now, at the age of fifty-two (Mary Louise) and fifty-three (me), we are on another adventure with our friends Gini, Janice, and Pat.

"Remember that time we drove across the

country with Gini and Pat in that old Pontiac?"
Mary Louise said. "Some of the places we stayed
had smaller bathrooms than this."

"Can you believe we were still friends after
four weeks crammed into that ten-year-old car,
with a water hose that leaked—"

"And we patched it with bubble gum! You always had to sleep on the rollaway because you
were the smallest, Tina. You must have weighed
ninety pounds in those days. What do you weigh
now?"

"None of your business. Why do you think I
took up tap dancing? Let's see if we can unpack
our stuff."

"Wait," said Mary Louise, pulling an aerosol
can out of her tote bag. "Let me spray the draw-
ers with Lysol first. You never know what might
have been in there."

"OK, Ms. Germ Freak," I said. We often tease
Mary Louise about her fastidious habits. She's
the only person I know who actually sings the
entire "Happy Birthday" song while washing her
hands.

After unpacking in our crowded little state-
room, somehow finding room to put everything,
we collected our friends and headed out to get
some breakfast.

The *Smirnov*'s dining room was a bright and
cheerful space, with windows all around. The tables were set with linen tablecloths, blue and
white china, crystal glasses, and sparkling silver-
ware. Comfortable yellow wicker chairs comple-

mented red roses, freshly cut and fragrant in a vase in the middle of each table. We sat at a round table for five and waited for a waitress to come and take our order.

Gradually the other tables filled up, but there was still no one to take our order. A little jet-lagged and really hungry, I waved to a large dark-haired woman wearing some kind of naval uniform, who seemed to be in charge.

She strode over to our table and said in a deep voice, "*Ja?*" Her highly polished shoes seemed oversized as they reflected the light.

Hmm, I thought. A German wearing a uniform on a Russian ship? Oh well, just play along.

"Hello," I said. "We were wondering if we could get some breakfast."

"May I see your room keys?" she said, not smiling, looking at us as if we somehow turned up on this ship illegally.

We handed her the little cards that opened our doors and she nodded.

"Ahhh. You are the entertainment," she said. "You dance, *ja?*"

I almost saluted but stopped myself in time.

"Yes, we are the Happy Hoofers and we're really looking forward to this cruise." I hesitated and then timidly asked, "Could I ask who you are?"

She looked annoyed, as if we should certainly know who she was, and said, "I am Heidi Gorsuch, the ship's director of activities. You vill dance tonight after dinner, yes?"

"We're looking forward to it," I said, dredging up my best party hostess smile. "We're so glad to have the chance to perform on your lovely ship.

Is there anything else you would like us to do before our performance?"

"Like vat?"

"We could do lap dances for all the men on board," Janice said, and I could see she was just getting warmed up.

I faked a laugh and glared at Janice. "Oh, Ms. Gorsuch, she's just joking. We thought we'd mingle with the other passengers and get to know them. Sort of goodwill tap dancers."

"Is gut," she said, and I could swear she clicked her heels together before moving to the next table.

"Good going, Tina," Gini said. "We're stuck on a Russian ship with a cruise director who talks like a drill instructor, a cabin the size of a broom closet, and no food in sight."

Gini always says exactly what she thinks about everything.

"Relax, Gini," Pat, our peacemaker, said. "We just got here. Things will get better. Don't make such a big deal about it."

"Listen, happy face, I'm tired and hungry and in no mood to—"

"You want food," a sullen, blond waitress said, appearing from nowhere. Her name tag identified her as Olga.

"Do you have a menu?" Janice asked, smiling as only Janice can.

"No menu," the waitress said, and was about to leave.

"Please," I said. "How do we get something to eat?"

She pointed to a long table on one side of the

room that was now covered with food and platters, baskets and samovars.

"You go get what you want," she said. "You want drink?"

"I'd like some orange juice," I said, and my friends ordered the same.

"Could you put a little vodka in mine?" Pat asked.

Olga looked at her as if she had ordered a hit of heroin, then walked off.

We got in line at the buffet table, which was loaded with croissants, muffins and breads, scrambled eggs kept warm in a metal container, jams and butter and bacon, sausage, and waffles. A man stood behind the table ready to whip up any kind of omelet you wanted.

I was behind a woman wearing a pale pink sweater over a rather plain beige dress. Because I have this habit of talking to people wherever I go—it used to drive my husband Bill crazy—I said to her, "Looks really good, doesn't it?"

She didn't turn around, but said with a very pronounced British accent, "I'mnotveddygood-inthemorning."

"Excuse me?" I said, leaning forward to hear her better.

She exhaled a long-suffering sigh, and said more slowly, "I'm not veddy good in the morning. Pahdon me." She picked up her plate of toast and a boiled egg and walked to her table.

I felt boorish, crass, like an ugly American.

"I see you're making friends in your usual effective way," Mary Louise said, laughing.

"Oh, shut up," I said, recovering my dignity and asking the man behind the table for a salmon omelet.

We were just digging into the first food we had eaten in twelve hours when a loud whistle startled us and made us turn. Heidi, lips still pursed from her ear-splitting signal, stood at the front of the room.

"Gut morning," she said, clapping her hands together like the principal in a boarding school and arranging her face in what I'm sure she hoped was a smile.

"Velcome, velcome," she said in a loud voice to the startled passengers. "I am Heidi, your cruise director. Ve haf many fun things planned for you on this cruise and you *vill* enjoy them. Please ask me if you have questions. Our Russian crew will do their best to help you, but they sometimes have trouble with the English. Some of them are just learning their jobs. I'm sure you will be patient with them." From the look in her eye, I was sure she was giving us orders, not asking for our cooperation.

"I vant first to introduce our captain. Captain Kurt Von Schnappel."

A tall, grim-faced man with gray hair in a dark blue naval uniform stepped forward and surveyed the crowd in front of him. I couldn't help feeling that he disapproved of us and that saying hello was a distasteful part of his job.

"*Guten morgen*," he said. "Enjoy your voyage." He gave a slight bow and left the dining room. That was it. No friendly welcome. No "glad to see you." I assumed we wouldn't be getting an invitation to sit at the captain's table anytime soon.

Heidi watched him go, then motioned to the white-suited crew members. They stepped forward, their hands folded, looking down at the floor.

"Oh dear," Gini said under her breath. "What have we done?"

"Now I vould like to introduce the crew to you. First is Sasha, who is in charge of the dining room."

Sasha stepped forward, his eyes darting wildly from side to side, desperately searching for a way to escape. His uniform jacket was buttoned crookedly, leaving one side longer than the other, and his shirt tail was untucked in the back. His hair stuck out all over his head as if it were trying to escape. Surely no older than twenty-five, he looked as if he couldn't be in charge of a falafel stand on a street corner in New York City, let alone a dining room on a cruise ship.

"Next ve haf our chef, Kenneth Allgood from England, who comes to us highly recommended. He vill prepare many delicious Russian meals for you—but with a British accent—and you vill enjoy them."

"A British chef on a Russian ship," a man in back of us muttered. "What's his specialty— Spotted Chicken Kiev?"

I turned around and saw a handsome man about my age, with dark hair graying at the temples, at a table near us. He looked like a golfer in his seersucker slacks and short-brimmed cap. I smiled at him and he smiled back.

The chef stepped forward unsteadily, a cigarette dangling from his mouth, wearing filthy whites with a toque perched on top of his greasy hair. He looked about twenty-eight years old. He glared at the passengers.

"Geeez," Gini said in a low voice. "His mother must have been Typhoid Mary."

I tried to give her a stern glance, but I was also trying to keep from laughing. If I looked at Mary Louise, we would both lose it. Out of the corner of my eye, I could see her stifling a giggle.

Heidi introduced the waitresses, the desk clerks, and the kitchen crew, and then she said, "Ve haf a special treat for you on this trip. Ve are very lucky to have with us the Happy Hoofers from America, who vill tap dance for us tonight and every night of the cruise. Please stand up, Hoofers."

We stood up and smiled at the other passengers, who clapped rather halfheartedly. Who could blame them? This cruise was not turning out to be the polished, interesting, professionally run trip they had been hoping for. And, of course, they had never heard of us.

"Happy Hookers?" an old man at the table next to us snarled. "What kind of a cruise is this? I don't want to see a bunch of hookers."

His wife tried to shush him. "They're *hoofers*, dear, not hookers. You know, dancers." But he kept on grumping and snarling until she pulled him out on the deck. As she dragged him away, she said over her shoulder, "He's been this way since Hillary ran for president."

We had another cup of good strong coffee and looked out the window at the clear, sunny day brightening the clean, white deck outside. I was glad we were making this trip in June when the temperature would be in the sixties and seventies.

We walked out to the deck and leaned on the rail as the ship glided by little towns, with brilliantly colored red and blue and green church domes peeking over the treetops, people picnicking along the riverbanks, and fishermen who waved to us holding rods.

"If that's their idea of breakfast, I can't wait to see lunch and dinner. What a crew of misfits. Why do I have the impression I'm on the Russian equivalent of the *Titanic*?" Gini said.

"Let's throw Debbie Downer overboard right now," Janice said, grabbing Gini by the arm.

"Look on the bright side, Gini," Pat said. "How else could we get to see Moscow and Sᵗ Petersburg and the Hermitage Museum?"

"We'll be lucky if this crew can get us to the next town without running into another ship," Gini said. "At least we can look forward to seeing the White Nights at this time of year. I'll be able to take pictures twenty-four hours a day if I want."

"Think of this trip as a great setting for a documentary," I said.

"Riiiight. Look on the bright side," Gini said. "You're always such an optimist, Tina. You remind me of that Monty Python movie, *Life of Brian*.

Brian is nailed to a cross, and he says, 'Peter, I can see your house from up here!' Then he sings, 'Always Look on the Bright Side of Life.' "

That's all we needed to hear. We linked arms and sang the rest of the song, dancing and twirling on deck.

Passengers gathered around us, clapping and laughing as we did some time steps and high kicks.

Even Gini was in a good mood after our impromptu practice session.

Two teenaged girls bounced up to us. "Are you the Happy Hoofers?" asked the one with dark hair with pink streaks on the side, who looked about seventeen years old.

"We are," I said. "Do you like tap dancing?"

"Oh yes," she said, "It's cool. We saw a musical on Broadway with Savion Glover. I love that kind of dancing. He has so much energy."

"We want to be your groupies," the younger one, around fourteen with curly blonde hair, said. "We saw you on YouTube, and half our class is taking tap dancing now. We could help you with scenery, or costumes, or anything you need. I'm Andrea and this is Stacy."

"We don't really have scenery and we already have costumes, but you're welcome to watch us rehearse," I said. "We'll teach you some steps. What are you doing on a cruise ship in Russia anyway?"

"Our grandmother brought us. She's celebrating her eightieth birthday and she thought it would be more fun if she took us with her."

"And I was right," an older woman said, coming up to join us. She had a face she had earned after eighty years of a good life—beautiful, lined, serene, ready for anything that came along. "Hello there, Hoofers," she said, and did a little time step and a ball change. "I'm Caroline. These are my two spoiled-rotten granddaughters, who are the joy of my life. Can't wait to see you dance tonight. I do a little tap dancing myself."

"Nana was one of the dancing Kennard sisters in the fifties," Stacy said. "She was really good, and she still is. She used to take us to Macy's Tap-a-thon every year in New York—that's why we love tap dancing."

"You're kidding," I said. "Mary Louise and I went every year for a while."

Her mention of the Tap-a-thons brought back all those hot August mornings when Mary Louise and I would drive into New York and put on some kind of cartoon T shirt—Mickey Mouse, Betty Boop, Garfield, whatever they thought up that year—and join people of all ages, colors, and states of mental health, to dance on Broadway in front of Macy's.

"Hi, Caroline," Mary Louise said. "We had so much fun at those Tap-a-thons. The best part was, after we danced, Tina and I would go to the fanciest restaurant we could find, still in our sweaty T shirts and tap shoes, and eat up all the calories we had just danced off. The last time we went, there were six thousand other people out there in Betty Boop T shirts and lace garters dancing on Thirty-fourth Street."

"We were part of the six thousand," Caroline said. "We were probably right in back of you."

"You would have pretended you didn't know us if you were anywhere nearby," I said. "We kept forgetting the routine and asking the trainer to do it over again. Then we figured if we made a mistake, who would notice? We had a great time. I don't know why they stopped doing them."

"They probably couldn't find anyone crazy enough to organize them after the woman who did them for years retired," Caroline said.

"Nana was always the best," Stacy said. "She helped the ones who were stumbling around. But the whole thing was really fun. I wish they still did it."

"Me too," I said. "Come on, Caroline. Show us what you've got."

Caroline smiled. She sang a verse of "Always Look on the Bright Side of Life" in a still-young soprano, breaking into a time step and grapevine that brought applause from the crowd that had gathered around us.

"How do you stay so young?" Mary Louise asked.

"These two girls are the main reason. And tap dancing is great exercise. My sister and I taught dancing until a few years ago. Then I decided to travel and have a good time. But I miss the dancing."

"Come watch us whenever you want, Caroline," I said. "I'm sure you could teach us a few steps—as well as a lot of other things. Here's my cell – call me any time you want to find us."

"I'll stay out of your way, but if you can put up with these two, they'd love it," she said, reaching out to hug her granddaughters.

"You got it," Mary Louise said. "They're welcome anytime they want to come watch us rehearse. We'll put them to work."

A young man with shoulder-length blond hair tapped Janice on the shoulder. He was about twenty-eight, around 5'10" tall, a little taller than Janice. His features were handsome, delicate. "Excuse me," he said, "but aren't you Janice Rogers?"

"I am," she said.

"I saw you in a play in Princeton one time. I always wanted to meet you. I'm an actor too. "

"Always glad to meet another actor," Janice said, her face lighting up the way it usually does when she gets to talk about the theater. "What play did you see?"

" '*Who's Afraid of Virginia Woolf?*' You were brilliant."

"That's a great play," Janice said. "I was lucky to get that part. What's your name?"

"Brad Sheldon."

"Are you working?"

"Sort of. I'm going to be in an off-Broadway production in the fall. A new play."

"What's your role?"

"I'm a schizophrenic medical student."

"You are not!" Janice said, laughing.

"I'm not kidding. Any help you can give me will be gratefully accepted."

"I'd like to try," Janice said, moving closer to the young actor. "This is a real challenge. I always think the gestures you make are an important part of defining your character."

"What kind of gestures do you think my schizophrenic would make?" Brad asked.

"I think he would use his hands a lot. He sort of talks with his hands. He'd get into the part physically—when he's excited, he'd move his whole body a lot and use his hands to make a point. Like this," said Janice, gesturing and reaching out to touch Brad while she talked. "See what I mean?"

"You're right," Brad said. "I've been so busy concentrating on saying the lines that I didn't think about my gestures. What else?"

"It's all about pretending you are schizophrenic. You should read up on that illness and figure out how it presents itself physically. Did you pretend to be different people when you were a kid?"

"Oh sure," Brad said. "Lots of times."

"That's all acting is . . . What did you say your name is . . . Brad?" Janice said. "The best actors I know just pretend they're someone else and have fun doing it."

"Is that what you do?" he asked.

"Of course. It's easy when you look at any part that way."

"This is really helpful," Brad said. "What else should I—"

The British chef, still in his stained whites, stepped in front of Janice. "Sorry to interrupt your acting lessons," he said to Brad. "I noticed you before when Heidi was introducing us. I'm Ken Allgood. Are you an American?"

"Yes, from New York," Brad said.

"Great city, that. I was there a couple of years ago and I'm going back as soon as I can. Maybe open my own restaurant. Best food ever there."

"Where did you go?" Brad asked, with an apologetic shrug to Janice.

We moved to the rail to admire the scenery, but we couldn't help overhearing the two men's conversation.

"All over. There was this one place—downtown somewhere. Right inside the door when you walked in there were all these apples—the smell was incredible. The dining room had dark red walls and an arched ceiling. And the food! Every mouthful was perfect."

"That sounds like Brigantine. I know someone who works there," Brad said. "I'll introduce you if you do get back to New York. Maybe he can get you a job."

"I say! You mean it? That would be great. We have to talk. What are you doing on this bonkers cruise ship anyway?"

"Well, I—I was supposed to come with my friend Maxim," Brad said, hesitating. He looked around the deck at the other passengers gathered in small groups, breathing in the clear, fresh air and talking to each other. "He's from Russia. He was going to introduce me to his parents. And he wanted to show me St. Petersburg. He said it was the most beautiful city in the world. He wanted to take me to the Hermitage and to Catherine Palace, and everywhere. We bought our tickets six months ago and then–" Brad stopped and turned away. There were tears in his eyes.

The chef touched his arm. "What happened?"

"He met somebody else. We lived together for a year and then he just left. At first, I wasn't going to go on this cruise, but I really wanted to see Russia because I had heard so much about it from him. But it's not the same. This trip would have been so great with him along. Now it just reminds me of him."

He stared at the river stretching ahead of us. My heart went out to this fragile young man who was obviously in so much pain. I was about to invite him to join us for some coffee later, but before I could say anything, Allgood put his arm around Brad's shoulder.

"Maybe I can help," he said. "Come on. I'll buy you a coffee and help you forget. We'll talk about New York. I still have some time before I have to get back to the kitchen."

Brad hesitated, then took a deep breath and smiled at the chef. "You're on."

"There's something about that Ken guy I don't like," Janice said to me. "I don't know why exactly, but I don't trust him."

"I know what you mean," I said. "He's got this sneaky way about him. Let's hope he can cook."

"Good luck on that one," the man who had been sitting in back of us at breakfast said. Up close, he was tall, and even better looking than I'd noticed in the dining room. He had one of those craggy faces—like Harrison Ford when he made the Indiana Jones movies about raiding lost arks. His hair was mostly brown with a little gray at the temples, and he was wearing the rimless glasses I love on a man. Bill used to wear them and so did my father. To me, they meant a man who is really smart, really in charge, really sexy. My kind of man.

"Hi," he said to me. "I'm Barry Martin. How did you get to tap dance in the middle of the Volga River?"

"Hello," I said. "I'm Tina Powell. My friends and I made a short video of our act and put it on YouTube. The agent for this cruise line saw it and hired us. We decided we were up for an adventure. What are you doing here?"

"It seemed like a good idea at the time," he said, smiling. He was even better-looking when he smiled. "I've been everywhere else but I've never been to Russia. Now I'm not so sure it was a good idea."

"You can't judge by the first couple of hours. Give it a chance. Maybe the food will be better than you think."

He looked at me and hesitated. I could see that he wanted to ask me something but wasn't sure if he should. I waited. I was feeling really good about myself that morning. I had on a light blue top that made my eyes look bluer, and my hair curved around both sides of my face the way it's supposed to when I use the dryer just right. I'd had it highlighted before we went on the cruise, so it was exactly the color I wish I had been born with. I could tell he liked the way I looked.

"Did your husband come with you?" he asked.

"My husband died last year," I said.

I swallowed hard. It's still hard to talk about Bill. I can't believe he's really gone. We married young—I was twenty-three and he was twenty-five. We both read everything that wasn't locked up, traveled whenever we had enough money, loved foreign films, saved every Friday night for a date, just the two of us, and never ran out of things to tell each other. I fell asleep in his arms every night for nearly 30 years.

"I'm sorry," Barry said. "You must miss him a lot."

"Every day," I said, the words catching in my throat. "He was my best friend."

"Did you say your name was Powell?" he asked. I nodded, and he said, "You know, there was a guy named Bill Powell in my class at law school. I don't suppose it's the same guy."

"Bill graduated from Yale Law School in 1982."

"It is the same guy. I knew him—not well, but I knew him."

I did a double take. "You're kidding. You really were in the same class with Bill? I don't believe it. Oh, we have to talk."

"How about right now?" Barry said, taking my hand. "Let's get some coffee."

"I can't, Barry," I said, torn between pleasure and duty. "I have to gather my troops and rehearse for our dance tonight. But I'd love to talk after our performance."

"Looking forward to it. See you then."

He leaned over and gently smoothed my hair back. Something I hadn't felt in a long time, that feeling that I wanted a man to kiss me, enveloped me, but I stepped back and said, "See you then."

Connect with  Us

Visit us online at
KensingtonBooks.com
to read more from your favorite authors, see books
by series, view reading group guides, and more.

Join us on social media

for sneak peeks, chances to win books and prize packs,
and to share your thoughts with other readers.

facebook.com/kensingtonpublishing
twitter.com/kensingtonbooks

Tell us what you think!

To share your thoughts, submit a review,
or sign up for our eNewsletters, please visit:
KensingtonBooks.com/TellUs.